The Gravedigger's Son

Also From Darynda Jones

CHARLEY DAVIDSON SERIES
First Grave on the Right
For I have Sinned: A Charley Short Story
Second Grave on the Left
Third Grave Dead Ahead
Fourth Grave Beneath my Feet
Fifth Grave Past the Light
Sixth Grave on the Edge
Seventh Grave and No Body
Eight Grave After Dark
Brighter than the Sun: A Reyes Novella
The Dirt on Ninth Grave
The Curse of Tenth Grave
Eleventh Grave in Moonlight
The Trouble with Twelfth Grave
Summoned to Thirteenth Grave
The Graveyard Shift: A Charley Novella

BETWIXT & BETWEEN
Betwixt
Bewitched

THE NEVERNEATH
A Lovely Drop
The Monster

MYSTERY

SUNSHINE VICRAM SERIES
A Bad Day for Sunshine

YOUNG ADULT

DARKLIGHT SERIES
Death and the Girl Next Door
Death, Doom, and Detention
Death and the Girl He Loves

The Gravedigger's Son

A Charley Davidson Novella

By Darynda Jones

1001 DARK NIGHTS

PRESS

The Gravedigger's Son
A Charley Davidson Novella
By Darynda Jones

1001 Dark Nights

Copyright 2021 Darynda Jones
ISBN: 978-1-951812-35-5

Foreword: Copyright 2014 M. J. Rose

Published by 1001 Dark Nights Press, an imprint of Evil Eye Concepts, Incorporated

Sign up for the 1001 Dark Nights Newsletter
and be entered to win a Tiffany Key necklace.

There's a contest every month!

Go to www.1001DarkNights.com to subscribe.

**As a bonus, all subscribers can download
FIVE FREE exclusive books!**

Acknowledgments from the Author

Thank you to Liz, MJ, and Jillian for giving me the opportunity to work with you! It has been such a pleasure and I can't wait for whatever comes next.

Thank you to my agent, Alexandra Machinist, and my very first editor, Jennifer Enderlin, for believing so much in Charley and the gang way back when dinosaurs roamed the earth. Has it really been over ten years?

Thank you to Chelle for the amazing edits. What a powerhouse you are.

Thank you to all of those behind the scenes at 1001 Dark Nights, the unsung heroes, for making us authors look like we know what we're doing.

Thank you to my amazing continuity editor, Trayce, and my amazing executive assistant, Dana, for loving this book and these characters as much as I do.

And as always, thank you, dear reader. You have made all my dreams come true.

Go Grimlets!

Author's Note

Dear readers,

Thank you so much for picking up this book! I am beyond honored to be writing it as a part of 1001 Dark Nights' amazing lineup. I have been in love with this couple for years and have wanted to write their story since their friendship first began, way back in *Fourth Grave Beneath My Feet*. They were just teens then, and a lot has changed, but I hope you love their story as much as I've loved writing it.

That being said, I want to clarify something before we begin. I, in no way, shape, or form, want to pretend I would know how Quentin, or any Deaf person, would *think*. I want readers to understand that, no, a Deaf person would very likely not *think* in English, even one born to hearing parents as my eldest was.

I've talked extensively with my sons about writing this book. My oldest was born deaf, and my youngest signs so well, he has been mistaken for being deaf/Deaf by many, even members of the Deaf community. They are as close as brothers can be. My youngest grew up interpreting for my eldest, starting when he was two. And believe you me, they didn't let that stop them for a minute. If there was trouble to be found, they were the ones to find it.

Just know that I am taking great liberties (artistic license?) with this aspect of Quentin's story. With my eldest's permission, and some of his insights, of course. To write the story otherwise would be impossible, but I want to acknowledge two things: the fact that a person born deaf would most likely not think in English, and the fact that this is not a Deaf story. Deaf stories can only be written by someone physically and/or culturally (capital-D) Deaf. I would never assume such a callous attitude concerning this rich and dynamic culture.

So, please forgive the liberties I take in writing Quentin and Amber's story. I hope you enjoy!

One Thousand and One Dark Nights

Once upon a time, in the future…

*I was a student fascinated with stories and learning.
I studied philosophy, poetry, history, the occult, and
the art and science of love and magic. I had a vast
library at my father's home and collected thousands
of volumes of fantastic tales.*

*I learned all about ancient races and bygone
times. About myths and legends and dreams of all
people through the millennium. And the more I read
the stronger my imagination grew until I discovered
that I was able to travel into the stories... to actually
become part of them.*

*I wish I could say that I listened to my teacher
and respected my gift, as I ought to have. If I had, I
would not be telling you this tale now.
But I was foolhardy and confused, showing off
with bravery.*

*One afternoon, curious about the myth of the
Arabian Nights, I traveled back to ancient Persia to
see for myself if it was true that every day Shahryar
(Persian: شهريار, "king") married a new virgin, and then
sent yesterday's wife to be beheaded. It was written
and I had read that by the time he met Scheherazade,
the vizier's daughter, he'd killed one thousand
women.*

Something went wrong with my efforts. I arrived in the midst of the story and somehow exchanged places with Scheherazade — a phenomena that had never occurred before and that still to this day, I cannot explain.

Now I am trapped in that ancient past. I have taken on Scheherazade's life and the only way I can protect myself and stay alive is to do what she did to protect herself and stay alive.

Every night the King calls for me and listens as I spin tales. And when the evening ends and dawn breaks, I stop at a point that leaves him breathless and yearning for more. And so the King spares my life for one more day, so that he might hear the rest of my dark tale.

As soon as I finish a story... I begin a new one... like the one that you, dear reader, have before you now.

Chapter One

If my calculations are correct,
I can retire five years after I die.
—True story

There aren't as many demons roaming the Earth's surface as one might think. Or, if one is a skeptic, there are a lot more. It all hinges on one's perspective. One's beliefs. But if Amber Kowalski's suspicions were correct, the bespectacled departed man standing over her was at least part demon. Half, maybe. A third, at the least. Anyone who woke up before the sun had to have a modicum of devilry in them.

"It's just, you have a big day ahead, Ms. Kowalski." He pushed his round glasses up with an index finger. "Lots to do."

Amber pulled the bedspread over her head. He tugged it back down until she could see over the edge. "Kyle, I finished the Wilkerson job last night."

"Did you get the money shot?"

"If by *money shot,* you mean did I take a picture of Mr. Wilkerson taking the trash out at midnight so he could sneak into his basement and watch porn? Yes. Yes, I did."

"He's not cheating?" Kyle sank onto the bed, disappointed.

"Nope. Not unless you're one of those people who think looking at porn is a form of cheating."

"I thought for sure he was cheating."

"You think everyone is cheating." She flipped the bedspread down and gave him a pointed look. "What happened to you?"

He snapped out of his thoughts. "Never mind. It's time to get up."

"Nooo." She covered her head again.

He tugged again.

"Kyle, I didn't get to bed until two. Wake me at seven."

"It is seven. Past, actually." He looked at the clock on her nightstand. "It's 7:14."

"What?" Her lids flew open. She glanced at the clock and scrambled out of bed. Her left foot got twisted in the sheets, and she did a hop-dance to get it out before hurrying to her bathroom. "Why didn't you wake me?"

"I did." He followed her but stopped when she slammed the door in his face. He knocked softly. Not all departed could do things like that. Tug at sheets. Knock on doors. But Kyle had been dead long enough to have learned a few tricks. "You have a client waiting in your office."

"At seven in the morning?" She shouted to be heard over the running water as she heated the shower.

"Yes. She died last night."

Amber cracked open the door and stuck out her head. "A departed?"

The pay sucked with departed clients, but this was her big chance. Her opportunity to make her mark on the world. Or the afterworld. Either way. Building her departed clientele was proving more difficult than she'd hoped. Nowhere to advertise. No one to give her business card to without it slipping through their fingers.

Amber was part private investigator and part psychic, for lack of a better term. Not a great combination, but the law firm from which most of her business derived didn't care about her extracurricular activities. They'd realized she was good at her job a long time ago. Well, three months ago. But it had taken Amber three months before that just to convince them to give her a chance. They'd been keeping a roof over her head and enchiladas in her belly ever since.

That was all she cared about. The roof over her gorgeous two-story Adobe, and the food this incredible town had to offer. She'd missed Santa Fe when she moved away for college. More than she would've imagined.

The rest of her income stemmed from rich widows wanting their cards read. Like her departed clientele, that part of her business was all word-of-mouth. She didn't advertise, but as with her PI biz, the clients started rolling in once she got established.

Thus, her big chance with this departed client. She showered at the speed of lightly toasted cinnamon bread and pulled her hair into a bun on the top of her head, ruing the length like she did every morning. She'd been threatening—no one in particular—to cut it off for years, and yet, she didn't.

Deep down, she knew why: Because *he'd* liked it. He Who Must Not Be Named. He'd always loved her hair. He would bury his face in it. Tell her it smelled like rain. Felt like water cascading through his fingers. The fact that she'd been keeping her hair long years after he left her a fetal, quivering mass of Jell-O irked Amber to no end.

It hadn't kept him here.

It certainly wouldn't bring him back.

She shook off the memory, the same one she had every morning about this time, and put on a cozy, shawl-collared sweater, leggings, and her favorite ankle-high boots—scrunched leather with a buckle. The sweater, like the boots, was a deep, bone black. They matched her hair. She used to wear a lot of cerulean to bring out the color of her eyes, but she'd gotten over that in college. Nobody cared what color your eyes were if you never made eye contact. Another habit she'd picked up after the impromptu departure of He Who Must Not Be Named. Another habit she was struggling to overcome.

"Coffee?" Kyle asked when she emerged from her fortress of solitude and walked the five-ish steps to her kitchen.

"Part of a complete breakfast." She popped a pod into the coffeemaker, pressed the start button, then gave her personal assistant all of her attention. Or, well, most of it. Some of it still lingered on He Who Must Not Be Named. She pressed her fingernails into her palms as punishment.

Kyle consulted the clipboard she'd never seen him without. The one he perpetually scribbled on. But he never seemed to flip the page or run out of ink, so what, exactly, he consulted was anyone's guess. She'd always wanted to ask how a clipboard and pen had ended up in the afterworld with him, but Kyle was a talker. She didn't know if she was ready for that conversation. Mostly because it could last for hours.

"Okay," he said, pointing at...no clue. "Besides Mrs. Rodriguez downstairs, Mrs. Harmon called and would like an emergency reading this morning."

By *called*, he meant that Mrs. Harmon had left a message on the machine, an ancient piece of technology she only kept around so Kyle could hear the incoming messages and report back to her if anything needed her immediate attention. Like, you know, a paying client.

Amber tried not to cringe. She failed. While Mrs. Harmon was her best-paying client, besides the Bristol and Partners Law Firm, the woman was also quite gullible. She'd been taken to the cleaners by countless charlatans and compared their *readings* to Amber's, questioning everything Amber told her.

One delightful piece of work named Starchild had garnered a special kind of hatred from Amber—an emotion she rarely entertained. She'd considered sending Kyle over to haunt her, but the charlatan would only use it as a ploy to get more clients. She would say she'd been contacted by the dead and was helping one of them *go into the light*. She would bask in the attention. She would probably even start a GoFundMe page for the departed's family. Aka, her pockets.

But enough about her. Today was a new day. Amber shook out of her thoughts and gave her messy studio a quick spruce, picking up cast-off articles of clothing, straightening books, and carrying a couple of cups to the kitchen. Then she turned back for a final inspection. The studio above her office wasn't much, but it was hers, and that was saying a lot in Santa Fe, New Mexico.

She popped the lid on her travel mug and turned to Kyle. "Okay, let's meet Mrs. Rodriguez, shall we?"

Chapter Two

Welcome to Madrid
Madrid has no town drunk.
We all take turns.
—Welcome sign

It was a risk, coming back to New Mexico after so many years away, but the demon Quentin Rutherford was tracking didn't seem to give a rat's ass. Based on news stories, eyewitness accounts, and the *compass*, a weapon the Vatican guard had given him, the asshole he'd been tracking for a month had set up shop in the small town of Madrid. Which was weird.

The town was a seat of mystical energy. It sat between Albuquerque and Santa Fe on a stretch of road called the Turquoise Trail. It was an old mining town turned ghost town turned hippie commune turned popular art colony. When he arrived, Quentin's skin fairly tingled with the energies swirling about the place. Like the wind before a dirt storm in the desert, hot and full of static electricity.

Still, last he'd heard, Amber was in New York. She'd gone to college there, a fancy one named Vassar. He didn't know much about colleges other than the one he attended for a whole year: Gallaudet University in Washington DC. He was there when all of his troubles began.

Well, more of the same troubles, but things escalated rapidly one fateful weekend, and his life had never been the same. His relationship with the elfin queen—his descriptor—had never been the same. The fact that he thought about her every day, craved her every day, meant nothing. He'd hurt her. Physically. Emotionally. Psychologically. There was no going back. And in all the years since, in all the towns and all the bars and all the women, he'd never met anyone who compared to the ethereal creature known as Amber Kowalski.

Ethereal. That was his new favorite word. He'd written it down in his notebook like he did all of the English words he wanted to remember. English was bothersome and clunky and didn't make sense, but that word *sounded* pretty. And the sign for it was almost as beautiful as Amber was. A befitting tribute to all that she was. All that she *is*.

"If you don't stop thinking about her, you're going to get us killed."

Quentin shook out of his thoughts, mentally flipped off the entity hitching a ride, and pulled his pickup off the main road that snaked through the tiny town. Madrid was a paradise for the chaotic-minded and a nightmare for anyone with OCD. Quentin leaned toward the latter. The town made him uncomfortable. Like his skin didn't fit right. And yet, the hodge-podge of mismatched buildings and displays was somehow alluring.

Brightly colored buildings dotted a sparse landscape. Most of the houses in town had been built for the miners in the twenties and thirties. They were small and tightly packed. The artists had transformed the town into a multi-colored expression of pageantry and wonder, like *Alice in Wonderland*.

Artisans traded their wares, but Quentin mostly cared about food—he was hungry—and the dead people—of which there were now three. Three dead people in less than a week in a town of two hundred? Barring a major accident, a plague, or a serial killer, it wasn't likely. Not in Madrid, pronounced *Mad*-rid, according to his source. This had to be the demon's latest stop. The demon he'd been tracking for a month. He kept missing the otherworldly being by a day or two. Hours even. Every time Quentin got to a hotspot, at least two people were dead, and the demon was gone.

And the activity was all over the place. The compass verified what Quentin and his *guest* already knew. The demon showed up, killed a few people, then left. To say that the activity was unusual would be an understatement. Demons craved stability. They possessed for a reason. They wanted to set up shop, kick off their shoes, and stay awhile.

Then there were those who would tear a straight path through a given area, leaving trauma and carnage in their wake. Again, this one didn't do that. It would be in New Jersey one day, Oregon the next, then show up days later in North Carolina. There was no pattern to its activity. No method to its madness. And that made tracking it a bitch.

When the compass, along with whatever natural-born talent Quentin had inside him, had tracked it to New Mexico, Quentin's pulse sped up with the possibility of seeing *her* again. It had yet to slow down.

It was bound to happen eventually. He would have had to come home at some point. The only home he'd ever known, anyway. At first, he'd taken solace in the fact that Amber was in New York. Now, he missed her more than ever, and a small part of him hoped she'd come home to visit her mom and stepdad. He just wanted to see her face. To touch her hair. To kiss her full mouth. But again, as hearing people would say: That ship had sailed.

"*You're doing it again,*" Rune said.

Rune, the demon inside him—and, no, not metaphorically—had possessed him while Quentin was in college. Rune was an old demon living in the bowels of the dorm. Quentin had felt him the day he moved in. During his second semester, he and a few friends, who'd sworn the dorm was haunted, took a trip to the nether regions beneath their rooms, and Quentin had come face-to-face with the ancient demon.

That was the last thing he remembered. He'd woken up two days later in the hospital with Amber, and her mother, Cookie, by his side. They'd flown up from Santa Fe, and he remembered how he thought she'd looked like a fairy princess from one of his video games.

At first, Quentin didn't think much about the event, other than to stay the fuck out of the basement. But the more time went on, the more he *felt* the entity inside him. A wiggling here. A settling there. Because of his abilities, he'd been possessed before. He did not like it. Turned out, Rune was different. An orphan in hiding, much like himself. He needed Quentin as much as Quentin unwittingly needed him.

On the bright side, Quentin had aced his history final. Rune had lived through it all.

That was about the time the Vatican came knocking. One day, he was home from school making love—at last—to the girl he'd loved for years. And the next, he was whisked off to Italy to begin training. It was the part of him he didn't recognize that'd made him accept the Vatican's offer. The violent part. The part he chose to block from his mind, unsure if it was the demon inside him or the darkness that had always lurked beneath the surface that made him hurt her.

"*Stop thinking about her already. We're hungry.*"

Quentin ground his teeth, got out of the truck, and walked to a coffee shop near the house he was there to scope out. A house that had a shop in the front part. A house that also had two police units parked in front, lights still blazing, and had been cordoned off with police tape. Cordoned. Another word he'd only recently learned. He liked that one for some reason.

"*The latest victim died only a few hours ago,*" Quentin said to Rune.

"*Yes. We hope we haven't missed him again.*"

"*Me, too.*"

The fact that the demon spoke better English than Quentin did irked, even after all these years. Of course, he'd been alive a lot longer than Quentin had.

It was still early, and he had his choice of tables when he stepped inside the small establishment—not that there were many. He stood eyeing a high-top near the front window where he could study the house. A forensics team was packing up. He would kill to get his hands on their report. Not that it mattered how the woman, a Dora Rodriguez according to a news report, had died.

Someone spoke to him from a short distance away. A woman. "Welcome to Java Junction."

He turned, and a redhead in her early thirties stood behind the counter, her brows raised in question. He stepped up to the counter and ordered an Americana.

"Room for cream?"

Even though he could hear her—in a way—he watched her mouth for backup. He shook his head. He'd gotten used to Italian coffee the consistency of motor oil. This would be nothing in comparison.

She punched a couple of buttons on the register. He liked the sound it made. The first time he'd realized that registers made a sound, he'd been so intrigued, the kid behind the counter had to tell him three times how much he owed.

"Are you shopping today?" she asked.

He shook his head again. "Looking into the deaths," he said.

"Are you Deaf?" she asked, in both English and ASL.

He cringed that she'd picked up on that fact so quickly and sagged in relief at seeing his native language. It was like dying of thirst and finding an oasis in the desert. "Yes," he both signed and said, making sure his voice was almost too soft for the woman to hear. "But I hear a little."

It was a lie. He didn't hear at all. What residual hearing he did have was about as useful as a sledgehammer at a tea party. *Rune* heard. The demon inside him. And through him, through the parasite who'd taken up residence inside his body, he could hear, as well.

He talked a little, too, though he tried to wiggle out of it every chance he got. Even though he could now speak reasonably well, he could also hear his voice. Again, through Rune, but he could hear it enough to know that it didn't sound quite right. It was too deep, maybe. And he didn't pronounce words correctly. He often missed the *S* sound at the end of plurals, never quite mastered the hard *G*, and don't even get him started on the *R*.

His relationship with Rune was an equally beneficial one. Quentin gave Rune sustenance and safe harbor. Rune gave Quentin the ability to hear and see at great distances. And they both had a profoundly honed sixth sense. They could both feel when a supernatural entity was nearby, which was how Quentin knew they hadn't missed the demon. Not yet.

"And you're here about the deaths?" the barista asked him before tugging her apron down to expose her cleavage.

He nodded. "I am. Anything you can tell me?"

"Are you an investigator of some kind? I mean, you don't look like a cop."

"I'm not a cop. I was hired by the family member of one of the victims." He'd told the lie so many times, he almost believed it.

"Really?" She leaned over the counter. "Which one?" Her signing wasn't bad. A little elementary, but he was impressed that she even tried. So few did.

"Sorry, that's confidential."

"Oh, of course." She turned to the side and looked out the window. "Three deaths in three days. That just doesn't happen here, you know?"

He could no longer see her mouth well, and discomfort prickled along his spine. Even with Rune's hearing, and her attempt at signing, he would rather see her face.

"Do you know how they were connected?"

She turned back to him, and he relaxed. "They weren't related, if that's what you mean. Mrs. Rodriguez had lived here forever. She drove a school bus. Even though they think she may have had a heart attack before she fell down the stairs, there was definitely something suspicious about her death."

"How do you know?"

She spread her hands before answering. "The cops have to get coffee somewhere, and we're the only coffee joint in town."

Joint. She said "joint" and did the sign for smoking pot. He laughed softly. "And the other two?"

"I know, right? Billy Tibbets was a glassblower. The only one in town. Took after his dad. So, he died first." She ticked the deaths off on her fingers. "His car shifted out of park while he was checking his mail." She shivered. "The second one, Angela Morrisey, was electrocuted in her bathtub when her space heater fell in." She eased closer. "What the hell? I mean, these houses are old, but damn. That is so against code, right?"

"It is." And no one in their right mind would prop a space heater over their tub.

"*Exactly,*" Rune said. "*But why these three people?*" Fortunately, no one but Quentin could hear the creature.

"*That's what we need to find out,*" Quentin replied.

When Rune first began speaking to him, Quentin worried that everyone would be able to hear him. They could not. Then he worried he was crazy. What was that saying? *The jury is still out?*

"Well, I'm Sarah," the woman said, giving him her sign name, an S on her right cheek. She held out her hand.

Quentin took it for a quick shake. "I'm Quentin." He didn't offer his sign name. It wasn't normally done in his culture until you got to know a person better. An amateur mistake, but he still appreciated the effort.

"And I guess I should do my job," she said with a schoolgirl giggle that belied her age. "Can I get you anything else?"

"*Bacon!*" Rune shouted in Quentin's head. Dude loved bacon.

Quentin pointed to a green chile and bacon breakfast burrito in the display case and said softly, "Burrito?"

She beamed at him. "Our specialty."

Quentin chose to ignore the fact that what she actually signed was closer to: *We give blowjobs.*

"Besides the coffee, of course," she added.

He gave her a thumbs-up and said, "Great."

"Will that be it?" When he nodded, she rang it up, took his money, and handed back his change. "Here you go, honey," she said, actually signing the word for *honey.* "How about you take a seat? I'll warm this up and bring it out to you."

He flashed her a grin, and she lingered a moment too long, the gaze transfixed on his mouth betraying her interest.

After a long moment, she nodded and said, "One Americana, coming up," before pirouetting away. She had pretty hazel eyes, but he preferred blue like the ocean on a summer day.

"You should hit that."

Quentin grabbed a seat at the high-top and refocused on the cops across the street. It had taken a long time for him to learn English. He was still learning, especially slang like *hit that.* But he was getting there.

Unfortunately, Rune refused to learn ASL. Probably for the best, though. It wasn't like Quentin could see him. He could hear and feel him, and sometimes, he thought he could even smell him—like smoke with a hint of brimstone—but he'd only seen Rune for that brief second in the basement years earlier.

Later, he'd asked Rune exactly what'd happened. How he'd ended up unconscious and in the hospital. Rune feigned ignorance. Quentin would get it out of him someday. But the longer they were together, the more fused they became. Quentin no longer knew where he ended and Rune began.

Sarah delivered the coffee in a mug that proclaimed *Bad Coffee Sucks* and set a plate down with the warm burrito while tugging at her apron again.

He gave her a grateful smile when Rune said, *"They're leaving."*

Quentin hadn't even been looking at the police cars as they headed out. That was another cool thing about Rune. He could see all around them and, just like with the hearing, so could Quentin. It was like having a three-hundred-and-sixty-degree view with video surveillance cameras.

The two of them drank some of the best coffee they'd ever had, scarfed down the burrito, left a tip, and walked back to the truck. The demon was nearby, but they couldn't tell if it was in the house Dora Rodriguez had died in or somewhere else close by. Of course, the fact that a woman snuck under the police tape, glanced around furtively, then walked around the back of the house just like Quentin planned to do did not bode well. If a demon was in the house, it would not take kindly to intruders. Even ones that looked like...like elfin queens.

Quentin stood by his truck in shock as he watched his ex. The same ex who was breaking and entering, two departed in tow, into the very shop he'd been surveilling.

Chapter Three

Here's a question for the mind readers out there.
—T-shirt

"There's a key under the pot."

After yet another furtive glance over her shoulder, Amber turned back to her newest client, Dora Rodriguez. The town of Madrid was tiny, and the residents kept an eye out for each other, but something strange was happening. Dora was the third person to die in as many days, and if the description of her attacker was any indication, a demon had caused her death.

Demons were jerks. No doubt about that. But they didn't usually go around killing humans. They liked to feed off them. Off their energy. Especially fear. Killing them served no purpose. Then, depending on the type of demon, the human would either go insane or die. Some demons, however, jumped from body to body, eventually leaving their host to live out their life with only vague memories of what had happened to them. Then there were the ones that used humans to cross into this realm, but that was a whole other story.

If this was a demon as Amber feared, then the entire town could be in trouble. More people could die, and the authorities would have no idea what was going on—or how to stop it.

Amber lifted a terra-cotta pot and found the key hidden beneath it. With shaking hands, she unlocked the aging back door. After a bit of shoving, she got it open.

"Yeah, sorry. It sticks."

"No worries," Amber said, trying to disguise the quivering in her voice. She did not relish the idea of facing a demon. She had a small arsenal of protective paraphernalia, but she did not have the capability to actually kill a demon. In fact, upon quick inventory of the usual suspects she had in her bag—salt, holy water, a cross—she realized that she was pretty much only capable of pissing a demon off. Great.

"Maybe we shouldn't do this," Dora said. She was a lovely woman in her fifties, shorter than Amber with lots of curves and a kind face. She'd given Amber the lowdown in her office that morning.

"I was working late, cleaning up the shop, when I heard something upstairs. I use the top floor for storage. It's more like a finished attic than an actual second story." She sniffed into a handkerchief and, once again, Amber wondered how it had made it into the afterworld with her.

Kyle stood off to the side, clipboard in hand. He patted Mrs. Rodriguez's shoulder, encouraging her to continue.

"Was it an intruder?" Amber asked the woman.

She shook her head. "I'm… I'm not really sure."

"I'm sorry, Mrs. Rodriguez. Go ahead. What did you hear?"

"No need to be so formal, sweetheart. Call me Dora, please."

"Dora. I interrupted. Please, continue. What did you hear?"

"It sounded like… I don't know how to describe it really. Like a scratching?"

Pins prickled across Amber's skin.

"Slow and steady, like someone was digging out from under the floorboards." The woman clutched her fists to her chest, clearly overcome with the memory. "I got to the top of the stairs and turned on the light. That's when I saw it."

Amber fought to keep her hands from clenching. The last time something had come out of the ground and grabbed her, she'd died for two hours. If she hadn't had a surrogate aunt named Charley Davidson, who just happened to be a god, she would still be in the afterworld. A place that was kind of wonderful. She'd felt safe and warm and loved. It was the getting there that was the hard part. The attack had been violent. Brutal beyond belief. The man had been so desperate to escape hell, he'd pulled Amber down with him. Ripping at her hair. Clawing at her skin. Beating her when she wouldn't help him until her life slipped through the cracks in her psyche and left the earthly plane.

She shook out of the nauseating memory and refocused on her client. "What did you see?"

"At first, just a blur. It barely registered. But when I turned toward it… Its face. It…" She made the sign of the cross and pressed her fingers to her mouth. "It wasn't human. *Madre de Dios*. It was a demon. I knew it the moment I saw it. Its face was contorted. Beastly. Gray and white and shiny. Like the flesh of a lizard. And the teeth." She shuddered.

Amber followed suit. At least the thing that'd attacked her had been human once. She couldn't imagine coming face-to-face with an actual demon.

Kyle glanced at her from over his glasses, his expression questioning.

She nodded. She would be fine. This was about their client. Not her.

"I don't know if he pushed me or if I just fell, but the next thing I knew, I was floating above my body at the bottom of the stairs. I saw the light, but I knew I had to tell someone. My niece will be in soon. I have to warn her!"

Kyle knelt beside her. "Mrs. Rodriguez, your niece found your body a few hours ago. I guess someone heard a commotion and called her."

Dora's hands flew over her mouth again. "Oh, no, *mija*. I didn't want that. Is she...? It didn't hurt her, did it?"

"She's okay," Kyle assured her. "She's upset, of course, but she's with her family."

Mrs. Rodriguez made the sign of the cross again and began reciting the Lord's Prayer.

Amber understood completely. The prospect of facing an actual demon made her knees weak. And yet, here she was.

"I'll keep watch," Kyle said, and Amber could hardly blame him. "I'll let you know if the authorities come back."

She nodded, drew in a deep breath, and entered Dora's shop that doubled as her humble abode. The back door opened into a kitchen. It was even smaller than Amber's but adorable. Bright colors. Lots of knickknacks. A retro diner feel. Dora was an eclectic artist, and her décor spoke volumes.

"The stairs are to the right," Dora said.

Amber wove around a turquoise table, fifties-style with Bettie Page placemats. She eased through a door and into a narrow hall. The stairs sat to one side of it.

Her pulse quickened, and she pulled her bag closer for something to hold on to. They navigated the hall to the bottom of the stairs. It was hauntingly unremarkable. There was no chalk outline like in the movies.

No bloodstain or broken glass. No fingerprint powder or evidence marker. Nothing to reveal the fact that a woman had died there.

Amber's phone dinged, startling both her and Dora. Dora put a hand on her chest, ironically to calm her racing heart. Amber took out her cell. Mrs. Harmon, wondering if Amber could fit her in. *It was an emergency!*

It was always an emergency with Mrs. Harmon. Amber fired off a text, telling her it would be that afternoon at the earliest, then put her phone on silent before stuffing it back into her bag. The bag, a conceal carry, matched her sweater. The same bone black but rather useless since she didn't dare carry a gun. She'd never been a fan. The last time she went to the shooting range, she'd ended up shaking so bad after the first few rounds, she'd had to stop from embarrassment. So, she kept her phone in the side pocket where a sidearm would normally go.

"Are you okay, hon?" Amber asked Dora.

"Yes." The woman's voice was soft with fear.

While Amber could see the departed and talk to them and interact with them, she could not touch them physically. Besides the cold, she could not feel them. They were not solid to her like they were to her aunt Charley.

But again…god.

Still, when they touched Amber, she *could* feel their emotions, and Dora had tried reflexively to grab her arm when her phone dinged. The woman's fear slammed into Amber's, compounding her emotions exponentially, but she didn't want to tell Dora to step away. The woman was scared, and Amber would absorb her emotions as long as she could.

He Who Must Not Be Named could feel the emotions of the departed if one of them touched him, as well. He'd always been able to. But for Amber, that ability had developed over time. And it wasn't a particularly *wanted* ability. But it came with the gig, she supposed.

When someone reached out of the shadows and grabbed her arm successfully, the fear that had been building to a tipping point almost strangled her. She screamed, figuring it was either the demon or a cop, as she turned to see a blond standing beside her. A tall blond. Scruffy and disheveled with at least two days' worth of growth on his jaw.

"What are you doing?" he asked, his signs sharp and edged with anger. The floor tilted beneath Amber's feet.

He caught her in his arms and eased her onto the second step. Once she'd settled, she pushed his hands away. He Who Must Not Be

Named stepped back, showing his palms in surrender, but his expression showed his irritation with her.

"Intruder!" Kyle said from behind him, a day late and a dollar short.

Quentin glared at him, and Kyle stepped back reflexively. Then he refocused his glare on Amber.

"What?" she asked, her hackles rising as hackles are wont to do.

"What are you doing here?" Again, his signs were sharp with irritation.

As Amber sat in utter astonishment—He Who Must Not Be Named was literally the last person on Earth she'd expected to see today—she used the break to take him in.

How much could a guy change in five years?

If Quentin Rutherford was any indication, a *hella* lot.

She barely recognized him. He'd hardened—in all the right places. His shoulders had widened more than most twenty-seven-year-olds. He'd always been muscular, even when they were kids, but either he'd been hitting the gym, or he'd been magically photoshopped. The hills and valleys that covered his body to exquisite perfection could be seen through the long-sleeved T-shirt he wore, his biceps stretching the seams to their limits. And the jeans, the ones with a few holes here and there, were not a fashion statement so much as a favored pair of work pants.

"Ms. Kowalski?" Kyle said.

Quentin turned to him, and Amber caught a glimpse of two things: the profile of his steely buttocks that had developed as much as the rest of him, and a particularly well-placed rip in the worn jeans that showed part of the indentation in his left ass cheek. The fact that he wasn't wearing underwear was a bonus. How could anyone she hated so much be so startlingly drop-dead sexy? Life was not fair.

Then she realized something. He'd heard Kyle. Quentin had turned when Kyle spoke, and she wondered if he'd finally gotten a pair of hearing aids. They'd never helped him that much before, so he never wore them, but technology had advanced a lot since then. Maybe they had more powerful aids now that could help him hear.

She snuck a glance but didn't see any mechanical earpieces. Interesting.

When he turned back to her, she couldn't get over how much he'd changed. His hair was shorter now and a little darker but still a rich, tawny blond. And he'd either started wearing it spiked, or he had bedhead. Either way, he was even more gorgeous than before. Full mouth. Straight nose. Deep blue eyes like the cobalt on a ceramic bowl.

Damn it.

He studied her as much as she studied him, and she cringed in self-consciousness. She scrambled to her feet on the stairs that allowed her to be a little taller than him and asked him, "What are *you* doing?"

"I asked first," he signed.

"This is Dora Rodriguez. She died last night." Amber signed and spoke at the same time to benefit her mixed audience. "She asked me to take a look."

Quentin turned and gave the perplexed woman a thorough exam. "Did you see it?" he asked. With his voice. His voice! No signing. And he spoke almost perfectly. But his voice was soft, almost impossible to hear, like he didn't want to speak too loudly. Regardless, she could hear the rich timbre in it, like warm honey over Amber's pitter-pattering heart.

She pressed her fingernails into her palms again. Enough. He was the one who'd left. He'd made that decision. She would not give her heart to him again. Not that he was asking, but just in case. She promised herself.

Dora nodded and pointed up the stairs.

Without the slightest hesitation, he reached up, lifted Amber off the stairs, and planted her on the floor in front of him. "Go," he said, his tone brusque as he headed up the steps she'd just been evicted from.

"What? No." When he turned back to her, she said, "You go. Dora is my client."

He pointed toward the second floor with his chin and signed, "Demon."

"Yes. I know."

He tapped his chest with his middle two fingers. "Demon hunter."

She blinked in surprise. Demon hunter? Like professionally? Was that even a thing?

It didn't matter. This was her case. She needed to see this thing through so Dora could cross over, and Amber knew exactly who to send her to when the time came. First things first, though.

She shoved past He Who Must Not Be Named—who would henceforth be known as He Who Shall Not Tell Her What to Do—and headed toward the attic.

He wrapped a large hand around her upper arm.

She shrugged it off. The demon probably wasn't even up there anymore anyway.

But when she crested the stairs, she felt it instantly. Damn it. Not the demon, per se. But the cold. Her breath fogged the air. She looked around at the boxes and bags of merchandise and supplies that occupied the area. Just as she turned to a hissing sound behind her, she felt him. He Who Shall Not Tell Her What to Do. Close behind her. His warmth as he pressed into her back. Wrapped an arm around her neck. Bent until his mouth was at her ear and whispered, "Shhh," just as the demon rushed her.

Chapter Four

Sometimes, I shock myself with the smart things I say and do.
Other times, I try to get out of the car with my seatbelt on.
—Bumper Sticker

Quentin tightened his hold to gain control of Amber completely and whirled around as the demon rushed them. The initial attack set fire to his back. He was thrust into the wall, barely able to brace himself with one hand, and knew he was out of his league. As the elfin queen struggled in his hold, he squeezed a fraction of an inch harder.

"Relax," he said into her ear a microsecond before she went limp in his arms.

He lifted her and carried her downstairs toward the front door, police tape be damned.

"*Hurry,*" Rune said in his head, urging him faster.

"*Friend of yours?*"

"*Not hardly. But he saw us.*"

Us meaning Rune. Quentin guessed that was bad. He got to the front door just as Amber started to come around. He fumbled with the doorknob but couldn't get it unlocked. He turned back to the woman. Dora?

She hurried forward and tried to open it, forgetting she was incorporeal. Her hand slid through the knob, and she looked at him, confused. "I don't understand why it won't open. It's not locked."

Quentin bit down and took his now-struggling package back through the house to try the back door.

"I can't leave," the man said—the dead one carrying a clipboard. "There's a barrier of some kind. I'm stuck!" The man was panicking, which was exactly what Quentin needed.

He ignored him and went to the door. It was immovable, too. Not locked. Closed from an outside force. *Fuck.*

"*Fuck is right,*" Rune said. "*Salt. Hurry.*"

Quentin felt Rune's urgency like a tidal wave of apprehension inside him. Rune had looked up, and through the demon's vision, Quentin could see the darkness descending around the house.

He looked at the woman. Her eyes were big and round, her fear palpable as his package began fighting him in earnest. He set the wildcat in a chair. Her hair had escaped the band on the top of her head. It fell in long, shimmering waves over her shoulders, and he stilled. She smelled like apples and felt like the sun on a winter's day, radiating warmth. And her eyes. That crystal-clear blue that he'd dreamed of every night for five years. What had Rune called that color? Cerulean? She still had a light sprinkling of freckles across her nose and on her cheeks. Barely perceptible. But it was the heart-shaped mouth, pouty like a doll's, that made his water in response.

Those lips thinned as she reared back and took a swing at him.

He easily dodged it, but she followed up with a left hook, clipping his chin. He grabbed her fist and glared at her.

"What the fuck was that?" she asked, forgetting to sign. He didn't need it, but she didn't know that. "You made me pass out."

"Ms. Kowalski," the man said to her.

She fought to get her fists back. "Kyle, now is not the time."

"No, you need to see this."

Quentin stood and turned on him, suspicion narrowing his eyes. But the minute he did, Amber gasped.

"Oh, my God," she said, jumping up. He turned back toward her, and she urged him back around with her hands on his shoulders. Then she yanked him back to face her as she signed, "Your back. He hurt you."

He was very aware. He just didn't know how badly. He'd never seen a demon like that. He'd barely caught a glimpse, but its colors and markings were unusual. And it was angry. Very, very angry. What was the word? Enraged? "It's okay," he signed to Amber. "We have to get you out of here."

"Me? What about you? You need medical attention."

He frowned at her—how bad could it be?—then walked to a full-length mirror the woman had in a messy craft room next to the kitchen.

Yep. Three slashes across his blood-soaked back. "Fuck. I love this shirt."

Amber blinked up at him in surprise. "You're worried about the shirt?"

He stared down at her, unable to believe that she was here. After all this time, she was right in front of him, so succulent he licked his lips involuntarily.

"*We understand now,*" Rune said. "*You did not tell us she is otherworld. We need to get her out of here.*"

"*Otherworld?*"

"*She is of us. She is passed over and come back, so she is no longer human. She just doesn't know that yet.*"

Guilt assaulted Quentin so hard and fast, it knocked the breath from his lungs. He'd seen her attack. He'd done everything in his power to stop it, but the priest had been too strong. Too powerful. He'd felt like a fly fighting a Mack truck. "*Then what is she?*"

"*She is otherworld. A traveler.*" Rune said the words like a lover. Or a stalker. Either way, he was getting far too familiar with the love of Quentin's life. "*Salt!*" Rune reminded him. "*It will come for us.*"

Quentin felt it, too. The demon creeping closer. Which, again, was weird. The demon had killed several times over, and now it was slowly creeping toward them? When it could attack and kill Quentin and Amber with the snap of its fingers?

Then again, maybe Quentin's reputation preceded him. That would be a nice change.

He pushed Amber onto the table, ignoring her appalled, "*Hey!*" and grabbed the satchel he'd tossed onto the floor when he first came in. He took out a jar of black salt and sprinkled it on the floor around the table.

"What are you doing?" Amber asked.

"Black salt," he signed. "And brimstone." He had to fingerspell *brimstone*.

"Brimstone?"

He lifted a shoulder. "Sulfur. Brimstone sounds cooler." It was another favorite word of his. He remembered it from when Amber had died. When hell rose to get the priest attacking her. He'd never forget the scent. Rune had told him years later that it was brimstone, and it had stuck. He'd written it down and prayed the priest was still choking on it to this day.

"Salt really works?" she asked.

"Depends on how my luck is going."

She raised a wing-shaped brow. "Have you seen your back?"

He tossed her a playful glare. It was like they'd never been apart. Life with Amber was always so easy. Comfortable yet intense. Joking in between longing looks over steaming cups of coffee. And even now, he fell right back into their routine. Their banter.

"You want in here?" he asked the two departed.

They stepped into the circle before he closed it and then hopped onto the table with Amber. The man with the clipboard—Kyle?—had to push his glasses up his nose after the jump.

The woman looked at Amber. "I'm sorry I got you into this, Amber."

"What? Dora, this is not your fault. This was a horrible thing that happened to you."

The woman nodded, unconvinced, then looked up, her face full of concern.

Amber pulled her knees up under her chin, and Quentin longed to tell her the floor was lava like he used to. They were kids then, and now was hardly the time, but it had been a favorite game of theirs.

"Quentin?"

He stopped setting items on the table and turned toward her. She looked like a little girl, hugging her knees. She started to say something then seemed to change her mind.

Worried the rickety table wouldn't take their weight, Quentin sat on it anyway, scrounging up the courage to do what he had to do next.

Amber turned to him and signed, "At least your shirt matches your jeans now."

He looked down. "I like these jeans."

"I do, too." When he tossed a curious gaze, she said, "I mean, I like jeans. You know, in general. It's just, yours have seen better days." She poked a finger into a hole, her touch igniting him instantly. It was the wrong thing to do, and she knew it. She jerked back her hand and continued hugging her knees.

He gave his jeans another once-over.

"*She is a traveler. The demon will crave her.*"

He stilled and asked Rune, "*In what way?*"

"*Her soul would taste like forbidden fruit to him.*"

Quentin didn't quite understand. "*So, like illegal fruit?*"

"*No, it would taste like something succulent he can't have. He shouldn't have.*

But he will not be able to help himself."

Quentin hopped off the table again, frustrated. "*Fucking English. Just say that, then.*" He took out what amounted to his only two weapons. The compass, which did way more than just give directions, and the dagger. "*Is she what is luring him closer?*"

"*Hard to say. He has seen us, too. And he has no reason to leave yet. He's looking for something.*"

"*What?*"

"*His car keys. How should I know?*"

Quentin ground his teeth. "*You don't have to be a smartass about it.*"

"*Sure, we do. We are frustrated. And this demon is a dick.*"

"*Aren't you all?*" Quentin could practically feel the glare coming from his rideshare.

"What are you going to do with that?" Amber asked, her voice more lyrical than he imagined it could've been. It was soft and tinkling like wind chimes. She gestured toward the knife.

He decided to play Russian roulette by balancing it on his palm, flipping it, then sliding it back into its sheath. "Hopefully, not a damned thing."

"How are you hearing me?"

He tripped over her words, then asked, "What do you mean?"

She tilted her head to one side to look into his face. "I didn't sign that. You heard me."

He tensed and chastised himself. He hadn't even noticed. He was so shaken by her. So stunned. Like that kid Charley Davidson had rescued that dark night over a decade ago. The first time he saw Amber, he fell. She was gorgeous even then. Even as a skinny kid with tangles down her back. But it was her personality. Her... He dug out his notebook and flipped to the page he wanted. Her *effervescence*.

She frowned and tried to read the notebook, so he slapped it closed and returned it to his back pocket. "And how can you talk so well now?" she asked, undeterred.

"Speech therapy," he said, signing the words.

"Bullshit." She signed it. Of course, she signed it. It was one of the first words he'd taught her.

"What did you mean earlier," he asked, changing the subject, "when you said Mrs. Rod..." He stumbled over the woman's name and gestured toward her. "She is your client?"

"Mrs. Rodriguez, Dora, came to me this morning. I'm a PI now.

She hired me to look into her case."

"Like Charley?" Quentin asked, his surprise evident on his face, he was certain.

Amber beamed at him. "Maybe someday. She helped a lot of people."

"She's a god. Or have you forgotten?"

"No, I haven't. But thanks for reminding me how inadequate I am." Before he could reply, she said, "You couldn't have cordoned off an area with access to a bathroom?"

He stuffed the compass into one pocket and a handful of black salt into the other.

"What does that do?" She pointed to the pocket with the compass.

"I have a few tricks up my sleeve. Just what were you planning on doing with the demon when you got here?"

Amber crossed her arms over her knees again. "I have a few tricks up my sleeve, as well."

He leaned closer. "Unless you have a rocket launcher in your pocket, I'd say you were screwed from second one." He held out the sheathed knife to her.

She straightened in alarm. "What am I supposed to do with that?"

"Use it, but only as a last resort. And whatever you do, don't cut yourself with it. It'll kill you." He leaned closer. "The goal is to kill him first. Then sheath the dagger."

"*Ay, Dios mio*," Dora said, making the sign of the cross.

He'd seen a lot of that at the Vatican. He'd never seen proof that it actually worked, though—unlike the dagger he was trying to give the elfin queen. It was a cursed dagger, but still.

"Why?" Amber asked. "What are you going to do?"

"Get us out of here."

"And how are you going to do that?"

He took out the rest of the black salt, pushed up his sleeves, and stepped out of the circle.

Amber jumped off the table and grabbed his arm, her skin warm against his. "Wait. What are you doing?"

"I'm going to try to contain the demon inside the house, then create a pathway for us to get out."

"You can do that?"

Her blue eyes gazing up at him stopped his heart. In all the years he'd known her, he'd rarely seen her wear black. It looked good on her, but he got the feeling it meant something much deeper. He could only imagine what his sudden departure had done to her. How it'd changed her, especially after all their plans. And how she was risking her life for a departed woman—someone who was already dead.

They would talk more, but right now, he needed to get her out of this house. He looked down at the hands clutching his arm, then backed up. "I can try."

She let go as if she'd been burned and wiped her palms on her pants. Straightening to her full height, she looked back at the dagger and then said, "You have five minutes."

"Then what?"

She grabbed the dagger. "Then I'm coming for you."

"I'll only need three."

Amber nodded as Quentin poured a salt trail around the entire kitchen. He did the same all the way around the first floor, creating one continuous line. He didn't know if his plan would work since the demon was upstairs and not down, but he had to try, even if it used the last of his black salt.

"He's…intense," he heard Kyle say to Amber. Rune could eavesdrop from several yards away. He waited to hear Amber's reply, but she said nothing.

Served him right. He'd hurt her, and she was taking his presence better than he would've thought. Then again, she was the most level-headed girl he'd ever met.

"I can't believe this," Dora said. "Why is there a demon in my house? How did it get in?"

Amber blinked and turned to the woman, dumbfounded. "Exactly."

Quentin wanted to tell Rune to stop spying, but he couldn't tear his gaze away from Amber if he tried.

"What are you thinking, boss?" the man asked.

Boss? Amber was his boss?

"Why is there a demon here?" she asked. "Of all places. What lured him?"

Dora gasped softly. "I cheated at dominos the other night, but only because that trollop Harriet Clooney cheats every week. I just thought I'd give her a taste of her own medicine. Do you think that was it?" She pressed both hands to her chest in horror as Quentin rounded a corner in the hall.

Amber fought a grin. She lost. "No, Dora. I don't think a demon has taken up residence in your house because you cheated at dominos. Unless, you know, the dominos were made from the bones of your enemies."

She cocked her head. "I don't think so."

Amber laughed softly then sobered. "I'm sorry this happened to you, Dora."

"Thank you, sweetheart."

Quentin stepped back into the kitchen, using the last of the salt in the jar. His shirt was soaked through, and he could feel blood dripping underneath it. He watched Amber watch him, her expression grim when she looked at his back.

She tore her gaze away and focused on Dora. "Can you think of any connection you might have to the other two victims? No matter how minute. How strange you might think it."

"Victims?"

"Yes, the other two deaths."

"Do you mean Billy Tibbets and Angela Morrisey?" She eased off the table. "But those were accidents. Wait. So was mine. Are you saying they were killed by the demon, as well?"

"No!" Amber jumped off, too. "I didn't mean that. I'm just saying there could be a connection."

"Ms. Kowalski," Kyle said as Amber inched closer to the circle, "be careful."

Dora put her hands over her mouth in horror and tried to step out of it. When she couldn't, she turned in a panic and started beating the invisible barrier with her fist. "Let me out! I want out!"

"Dora, please." Amber eased closer, showing her palms but not touching the woman, as though she were approaching a wounded animal. If Amber were anything like Quentin, the woman's panic would overcome her as well if she touched her. The emotions would transfer. "You have to stay inside."

Quentin inched closer. The situation could turn volatile in a heartbeat. The demon must've figured out that something was up. A blur swooped into the room and frightened the woman. She turned to Amber, her eyes wide with fear, and shoved with all of her energy.

And the elfin queen flew out of the circle and into the teeth of an ancient, angry demon.

Chapter Five

I'm not superstitious.
I'm just a little stitious.
—Meme

The force of Dora's fear hit Amber square in the chest. The air whooshed out of her lungs. She flew back, clipped one corner of the table, and expected to land hard on the floor head-first. Instead, she tumbled into a net of thick, suffocating blackness. The world tilted and turned as if she'd been caught in a tornado. Then, she was flat on a hard surface, looking up at a ceiling with exposed rafters, fighting to fill her lungs with air.

Quentin was on top of her at once. He pulled her into his arms and covered her body with his, just as the entity attacked. Holding her with one arm, he sucked in a sharp breath and fell to the floor.

"Quentin!" Amber shouted as the darkness shot toward them again.

He reached into his pocket and, first, tossed some of the salt into the air and, second, formed a thin circle around them, pivoting on his feet while holding her in his arms. Once the circle was complete, he took out a locket of some kind and waited.

The salt in the air dissipated the demon, but not for long. It reformed its energy and scurried to a corner, hiding behind a shelving unit to lick its wounds.

"That hurt it," Amber said, surprised, wondering if she could get black salt and brimstone on Amazon.

Quentin eased his hold, and she slid off his lap and onto the floor, careful to stay in the circle he'd made. But she felt something on her cheek. She touched it and then pulled back her hand. Blood. But not hers.

She looked at Quentin.

He was looking at her, too. He brushed the blood off her cheek with a thumb, then visibly relaxed and asked, "You okay?" He pulled her forward and patted her down, checking for injuries, but the only wounds she saw were on him.

Quentin now had a gash across his cheek—frighteningly close to his left eye—and three slashes on his neck. The skin around it was red and irritated, and blood ran from the gashes into the collar of his shirt.

"Quentin," she said, not sure what else to say. She lifted her sweater over her head, thankful she'd thrown a tank on underneath, and pressed it to his neck.

He took the opportunity to check her out further in the tiny space.

"I'm okay. It didn't hurt me."

They were back in the attic and now stuck in an even more confined area, Quentin on his knees and Amber on her butt with her legs drawn up.

"We have to get out of here." He signed it but also used his voice, the sound barely above a whisper. It was soft and deep and flowed over her like warm water. Then his gaze locked onto hers, and she wanted the water to rise and drown her.

Tears stung the backs of her eyes, and she pressed her nails into her palms again, trying to draw blood. After a prolonged moment, she tore her gaze away and looked toward the corner the demon had scurried into. She saw nothing but shelves of merchandise and art supplies, but she'd felt it when it grabbed her. Read it. Almost lost herself inside it like she sometimes did with her clients. "It's angry."

Quentin followed her line of sight and nodded. "I felt that, too."

"It's looking for someone. Waiting for someone. Someone it is very angry with." When Amber looked back at Quentin, he was staring at her mouth. She knew the feeling.

His lips were fuller than most men's, a masculine shape framed by a healthy dose of scruff a little darker than his hair. He snapped to attention and continued checking her out, running a hand down her back, searching for wounds.

"It didn't hurt me."

"No, it only abducted you. We have to get you out of here." He scanned the area, looking for an escape.

Two small, round windows allowed light in, one in the front of the cottage, and one in the back. But the cathedral ceiling had no other openings. No other routes of escape, even if they could get past the demon's barrier.

"We need to get back downstairs." Quentin was signing everything, using his voice minimally. And Amber wondered why, when he was so good at talking now. He bit down, working his jaw, then said, "I had a plan."

"To get us out?" she asked.

He hadn't been looking at her, yet he nodded. How? How was he hearing her?

She pulled back the sweater. His neck was still bleeding, so she pressed it against him again. "That salt seems to work well."

"Yeah, and that was the last of it." He frowned at her. "You're ruining your shirt."

"Sweater," she corrected. "And I don't care. Are you okay?"

Her question seemed to surprise him, and he signed, "Always." He'd said that to her so many times. That exact sentiment.

Will you stay with me?

Always.

Will you be there for me?

Always.

Will you love me?

Always.

And she'd believed him. To the depths of her soul. "It's hurt." When Quentin questioned her with a raised brow, she said, "The salt. It hurt it. I felt it. It burned like acid."

Quentin stilled and asked, "Did it hurt you?" Like he cared. Like her pain meant anything to him.

Remember who he is, Amber. "No. I'm fine. I told you." She struggled to get up, but he still had an arm around her waist to hold her inside the circle.

He stood instead and took her with him, lifting her to her feet as if she weighed nothing, then kept his hands on her to steady her. "How hurt is it?"

She brushed off his hold. "Very, but it could still attack."

"We're going to have to risk it." He sank onto one knee and signed, "When I break the circle, run."

"I didn't think the circle held us here."

"It doesn't, but I need the salt."

"Oh, right." Her pulse started to pick up speed.

"We need to get into the circle in the kitchen."

"Okay." She nodded, feigning confidence. "I can do that. Then what?"

He looked over his shoulder. "Told you. I have a plan."

She glared. "Well, is it a good one?"

One corner of his mouth crept up suspiciously. "Always."

She tossed her sweater to the side, readying to run, but reminded him, "You clearly don't remember the time we skipped school and went to look for the Blue Lady in the cemetery."

"Right." He winced. "Okay, besides that time."

She drew in a deep breath. "Just say when."

"Now." He said it so softly, she almost didn't hear, but the minute he broke the circle by scooping some of the salt into his palm, the demon darted out from behind the shelves.

She panicked and bolted toward the stairs, taking them three at a time, sparing only a quick glance over her shoulder about halfway down. It was the wrong thing to do. She almost pitched forward when she tried to stop. She had to grab the balustrade to stop herself as she looked back.

Quentin stood motionless as though waiting for the demon to attack him. Yet he watched her. Gave her time to make her escape. A microsecond before the darkness raked across him, he let the salt go, flinging it into the air and at the entity.

It still sank its claws into him.

He flew back against a wall, almost knocking the house down, then ran for the stairs. He took nearly the entire floor in one jump, grabbing Amber along the way and scuttling into the kitchen. He propped her onto the table. She'd never felt so much like a ragdoll as she did today.

Then, he sank to his knees beside the table and fell under it.

"Quentin!" She scrambled off the top and crawled underneath with him. He doubled over and held his head with both arms. "Quentin, what did it do?"

He shook his head and rocked, and when she touched him, carefully placing a hand on his shoulder, he exploded. One second she was under the table with him. The next, the table crashed against the refrigerator, and she was looking up at a ceiling again, pressure on her throat.

He pinned her to the floor, his teeth clenched, his forearm pressed against her throat.

"Quentin," she choked out, but his blue irises had turned black. No. Not just his irises. His eyes in their entirety. They'd literally turned black as she watched. Tendrils of ink sprouted from the corners and covered the white and blue. He looked...possessed.

"Why are you here?" he asked, his voice deeper than before. Animalistic. Preternatural. And then he stopped. Blinked. Shook his head as though trying to clear it before looking back at her. "Traveler."

She tugged at his arm and tried to summon some of the moves she'd learned in self-defense class, but all rational thought had fled the building. So, she decided to state the obvious, her voice strained. "Quentin, I can't breathe."

He let her go instantly, released a growl of frustration, and turned away from her.

She rolled over and lay in a fetal position as she coughed and tried to fill her lungs. Her cheeks, hot and wet with tears, burned almost as much as her throat did. She coughed until she gagged and almost threw up on Dora's floor. The departed woman stood over Amber, her face brimming with concern.

Kyle was still there, as well. "Ms. Kowalski," he said, kneeling beside her, clutching his clipboard tighter to his chest. "What can I do?" He tossed a glare over his shoulder.

"Nothing," she said through a few more coughs. She sat up. "I'm okay. Really."

Dora held her fists over her mouth. "*Mija*, you're covered in blood."

She looked down. Blood did indeed cover her tank, but it wasn't hers. "Quentin!" She scrambled closer to him but didn't dare touch him. He'd changed more than she could've imagined.

He jerked away and kept his back to her.

"Stop being an ass. Turn toward me."

He eased farther away when she tried to see around him. He'd been hurt. Badly.

"Either turn toward me, or I'm stepping out of the circle, getting my phone, and calling for help." She hadn't wanted to bring anyone else into the situation, but things had escalated far beyond her comfort level. As a former angel, her stepdad would know what to do.

Quentin's head swiveled sharply toward her, anger evident in his moves. His every breath.

"That's what I thought," she said, satisfied. "And you can just shove that attitude up your ass."

He glared at her, then looked at her throat. Guilt washed over him. She could see it in every line of his exquisite face. His eyes were blue again. A little darker than before, perhaps, but blue with a white sclera. Oh, yeah. They definitely needed to talk. But for now, the demon had clearly tried to rip him in half.

Amber leaned around him and tried to suppress a gasp. More slashes ran along his stomach and rib cage. His shirt was now more red than blue, the front soaked through, the viscous liquid seeping into his jeans. "Oh, Quentin." She tried to raise his shirt, but he didn't let her.

He covered his stomach with an arm and struggled to his feet.

"Wait, Quentin, wait." She stood, as well. When he looked down at her, she put a hand on his chest. "We have to bandage this." There was so much more blood this time. They had to get him to a hospital.

He shook his head and signed, "I'm okay. We have to get out of here."

"I'm all for that." The faster they got out, the quicker she could get him to an emergency room. The closest was probably Santa Fe. "You had a plan?"

He stepped around her, and she saw how he'd drawn the black salt on the floor. He'd created an outer circle around the entire house, then, at the back door, he'd drawn two straight lines, the width of the door, that connected the inner circle they stood in, to the outer loop around the house. The circle that had been around the table. The table now sat upended on the other side of the small kitchen, but the salt ring had miraculously remained unbroken.

He stepped to the part of the circle with the two lines drawn out from it and glanced at her over his shoulder.

Dora made the sign of the cross again and clasped her hands together.

Kyle hugged his clipboard.

Amber stood too close to both of them. Their emotions mixed with hers, and she didn't know if terror actually filled her or if it came from her two friends. Probably a little of both. Without her sweater and with her tank now soaked with Quentin's blood, she started to shiver. It wasn't cold out, but it was just chilly enough to cause gooseflesh to sprout over her skin. Then again, that could've been the terror.

Quentin grabbed the dagger that had fallen just across the circle, drew in a deep breath, and broke the line by swiping his boot through it.

They waited, all four of them looking up, listening intently for any rustling sounds.

When all remained quiet, Quentin stepped into the little corridor he'd created to the outer salt line that ran parallel to the door. He turned to her. "This should contain the demon inside that part," he signed and spoke simultaneously, pointing to the new enclosure he'd created. Again, his voice was so soft and deep, he was hard to understand, and Amber was beginning to believe he did it on purpose. As if he were embarrassed by the way he talked.

He unsheathed the dagger, dipped the toe of his boot into the salt near the door and then dragged it across, breaking the line.

They waited again. Nothing. And Amber released a breath. "The door?"

He tried it. The knob turned, and he slowly cracked it open. Dora and Kyle rushed through, not waiting. Amber could hardly blame them. But she and Quentin couldn't get out of the crack he'd created.

The door pushed the salt along the floor as it opened, and he was careful not to break the barrier he'd created for the demon by widening it ever so slowly. When he opened it enough for them to squeeze through, he stepped back through the short corridor and gestured for her to go ahead.

"Oh. Right. Like last time?" She planted her fists on her hips. "You get to sacrifice yourself while I get away?"

A rustling came from upstairs, and she tore out of the house at the speed of light. If he wanted to sacrifice himself, fine. She was not waiting around. But she did stop, turn around, and watch as he grabbed the satchel that he'd brought in. It required him to step into the *bad part*, and Amber lunged at him when darkness entered the kitchen.

She grabbed Quentin's arm and pulled.

He was right there with her. He rushed through the door, dragging her with him, then turned back and closed it.

Amber clung to him as if her life depended on it. Then, realizing her mistake, she jumped back from him and hugged herself. "Are you okay?"

He put the dagger back into the satchel and draped it carefully over his shoulder. "I'm okay," he signed, suddenly unwilling to look at her. "We need to get cleaned up."

"We need to get you to a hospital."

"No. I can't risk losing this one. I've been tracking it for a month. It's been all over the place. I won't get another opportunity like this." He started walking toward the main road, clutching his stomach.

It was still early enough that only a few people were out. Oddly enough, they didn't notice a bloody man with an Indiana Jones-style satchel, walking along the highway toward a dusty black Ford Raptor. Strange, that.

"Quentin, we look like we just walked out of a horror movie."

He kept walking, unfazed.

"Quentin Rutherford. I know you can hear me. What do you mean?" Amber hurried to catch up. "How have you been tracking a demon for a month? How do you track a demon at all?"

"Later. I need to change and get back in there."

"What?" she screeched, the sound not unlike a barn owl.

They'd reached the black truck parked just off the main road. Hopefully, it was his since he opened the back door and was rummaging through a duffle bag inside. "I need food. It will help me heal." Instead, he grabbed a handful of painkillers, unscrewed the top of a whisky bottle, and downed them. Amber's stomach hurt just watching it.

"So now you're Superman? You have super healing?"

He put the whisky away and pulled out another long-sleeved T-shirt, this one a faded salmon color, one of her favorites. "Something like that."

Holy cow. She hadn't been dreaming. Or hit on the head. Well, yes, she'd been hit on the head, but it hadn't caused a hallucination. His eyes had really turned black. Her knees weakened, and she leaned against the door for support. "Does your healing have anything to do with what's inside you?"

He stopped, his jaw flexing in annoyance. "Something like that."

She slammed her lids shut, every scenario imaginable running rampant through her mind. When she opened her eyes again, she looked around and saw Kyle and Dora standing close by, their expressions worried as though unsure of what to do.

Quentin opened a first-aid kit, found a roll of bandages, and gingerly lifted his shirt over his head.

Another wave of lightheadedness washed over her. The slashes on his back were so much deeper than she'd thought they were.

He took the bandage roll and started to wrap it around his torso without a single drop of Neosporin.

"Stop." She took the gauze out of his hands and stepped around him to look in his kit. She found antiseptic spray. It wouldn't feel good, but he seemed perfectly able to work past the pain.

She turned to him and finally saw his stomach. His rock-hard abs, the muscles ripped. But she could've sworn she saw a rib peeking out of his side.

The world spun. She fought off the wave, took a towel and a bottle of water, and started cleaning the blood off him, readying to apply the spray.

He sucked in a sharp breath when the cold water hit him, then signed, "I don't have time for this."

"Make time. This must be disinfected, at the very least." She could only pray he hadn't been lying about his ability to heal quickly. Charley had been like that. The last time Amber had seen Quentin, he had been nowhere near Charley's caliber of being. Clearly, a lot had changed.

Thankfully, the only people who would be able to see them were the ones in the house immediately to their left. The door blocked the other side well, but it would be a small miracle if the police weren't called.

Amber cleaned his wounds the best she could, her hands shaking. Whether from the chill in the air or the fact that her ex had been ripped to shreds by a demon, she couldn't say. She finished by drying Quentin off, then reached up and cleaned the gash in his cheek, as well. The bleeding had stopped, even from the deepest cuts. She'd never felt the demon's claws. It didn't escape her how lucky she was.

He watched her from beneath thick lashes, his blue eyes trained on her face as she sprayed the gashes with the antiseptic. He sucked in another sharp breath. For the one on his face, she took a piece of gauze, sprayed it, and blotted his cheek.

He shouldn't even be standing, and yet he stood there as if he'd barely had his bell rung. Whatever—*whoever*—was inside him was powerful. At the moment, she decided to be grateful for that fact. But still, watching him in pain, in such agony, was almost more than she could bear. A lump formed in her throat as she thought about it, and she fought the quivering of her lower lip.

"This is so bad, Quentin."

"I've had worse," he said, his voice barely audible.

That was when she saw the thin scars across his back, chest, and arms. Were those once like these had been? Did he really heal so well that his scars were almost imperceptible? She motioned for him to hold up his arms. He lifted them, and she began wrapping the bandage around him, tight enough to hold him together but not so tight that it cut off his circulation. He needed about a thousand stitches, but this would have to do for now.

"Do you have extra pants?" she asked when she finished wrapping the wounds. The blood had soaked the front of his jeans.

He gazed down at her for a long moment and then, without fanfare or ceremony, started undoing his belt buckle. He kept his hawklike gaze on her as he unfastened the button and split the fly open.

Too late, she remembered that he wore no underwear. She whirled around, but not before she got a rather good look at the exquisite package he carried between his legs. His body wasn't the only thing that'd grown up.

Chapter Six

On the bright side, I'm not addicted to cocaine.
—T-shirt

Quentin almost laughed when Amber turned away from him. Her cheeks turned pink instantly as he kicked off his boots and slid his jeans over his hips. Normally, he wore boxers, but the trip had taken longer than expected. He had yet to hit up a laundromat. He did wonder if he shouldn't have checked the windows around them before stripping. Then again, if anyone was going to call the cops, they would have already. The houses closest to them either weren't occupied at the moment, or the occupants were out and about.

Still, it was getting pretty late in the morning. Most of the businesses were open, and several tourists walked through town.

Quentin found another pair of jeans and hopped into them, regretting the hop instantly as his stomach muscles contracted. Pain shot through him as if a nine-millimeter had sprayed him.

"*Smart,*" Rune said.

"*Shut up.*" He let his gaze travel over Amber's elfin profile. Down her shapely neck. Over her delicate shoulders. Her long hair cascaded, luxurious like silk, to the top of her incredible ass.

He'd dreamed of her every night for years, and here she was, right in front of him. But he was the last thing she needed. He'd almost killed her once today already. She should get as far away from him as humanly possible, no matter how badly he wanted to bury his face in her hair and his cock in her—

"*We're going to find a better apartment. One without that constant whining sound.*"

Quentin finished buttoning the jeans and pulled on a long-sleeved T-shirt as another virtual spray of nine-millimeter bullets hit him, then sent Rune a mental, "*Fuck you.*"

"*She is a traveler.*"

"*And?*"

"*She is way out of your league.*"

Quentin scoffed as he tugged the shirt into place. "*She was out of my league long before she became a traveler.*" He reached over and tapped Amber on the shoulder. When she turned around, he presented himself to her. "Better?"

"Much, but you still need a hospital." Her cheeks were still pink.

"I need food." He looked at the coffee place where he and Rune had eaten breakfast, but he wanted something meatier.

"I'm parked at the Mine Shaft Tavern." Amber looked at her watch. "Great food, and they should be opening in a couple of minutes."

"Sounds good." He made sure to sign as much as possible. She didn't need any more proof of what a sideshow attraction he'd become. He may be able to talk fairly well now, but he still stumbled on words. His voice was still wrong. He didn't sound like other people, and he sometimes got the odd looks to prove it.

She looked down at her blood-soaked tank top. "I can't go in there like this." She studied the road. "It's only a couple of minutes' walk. I have extra clothes in the trunk, but my bag is still inside the house." She turned back to him. "The same bag that has my keys and my phone in it."

"We'll call a service to get you a new set. I'll have your bag sent to you when this is over."

"I'm not leaving, Quentin." She stepped closer and put a hand on his arm. Warmth radiated out of her fingertips and over him. "I want answers. And, quite frankly, I don't give a shit if you want to give them to me."

He bit down, frustration taking hold. He'd never been this close to capturing this demon, and he had it trapped. For now.

"*That's not it,*" Rune said. "*You don't want her to know about us. About what we are.*"

Quentin ignored him. "You can't go in there looking like the final girl from *The Texas Chainsaw Massacre*." He noticed the shivering. "And you're cold."

"I'm fine. I just—"

He turned his back and rummaged through his duffle bag again. He found an old T-shirt that had been too small for years, yet he took it everywhere. She'd bought it for him when they were in high school. Dark gray with a white skull as if it had been spray-painted on. He'd loved it and wore it almost every day for a year while at Gallaudet. He'd missed her so bad. And then… His world changed entirely.

"*We changed your world,*" Rune said. "*You gave her up for us.*"

"*Like I had a fucking choice.*"

"*Need I remind you, human, you did.*"

Quentin drew in a deep breath and held out the shirt to her. "*No, Rune, I didn't.*"

Rune forewent a smartass comeback—for once—and said simply, "*We are grateful.*"

She shook out the shirt and drew in a soft breath when she recognized it. She pretended not to and started to pull it over her head.

"No," he said, gesturing toward her tank top. "That needs to come off."

Her beautiful eyes rounded, and she glanced around. "I can't strip here. Someone will see me."

Instead of *remove clothes*, she did the sign for *stripper*, and Quentin tried not to laugh. "I just got naked. Didn't bother me."

"Clearly, you're used to living like a hobo."

He felt his brows snap together. "Hobo?"

She fingerspelled it for him, then realized that wouldn't help. "You know, like a transient. A person without a home."

"Oh, right," he signed. "Homeless."

"Yes. Sorry. I didn't mean… That was a bad joke."

At least she was joking with him and not trying to claw his eyes out. She had every right to hate him. He reached over and tugged at the shoulder strap on her tank. "Off."

"Fine. Here." She took a jacket off the seat and handed it to him. Then she traded places with him, brushing past him and sinking farther into the corner between the truck and the door. "Hold that up. And turn around."

He did as ordered. What she didn't know, however, was that he had a three-hundred-and-sixty-degree view through Rune. It wasn't quite the glaring technicolor of a human's vision—the colors muted to shades of blues and grays—but it worked. When she lifted the tank over her head, her delicate skin covered in goose bumps, he couldn't have looked away if he'd been paid to. She was breathtaking, every curve filled to exquisite perfection. She wore a black bra and had cleavage now. That was new. And titillating.

His pants tightened in response, and he chastised himself for being such a whore. Especially now. Because that was what Amber needed. Him ogling her like a stalker. Getting hard like a pervert.

She used some of the water and a clean towel to wipe some of the blood off her incredible skin, and he tried to block out the image. But closing his eyes didn't help. Rune was in his head. So, he concentrated on what he would do next.

First and foremost, he needed food. Amber had been right. He did heal super-fast, again through Rune, but they both needed sustenance to do it. Soon, however, he would hardly be able to move. The soreness would set in, and he would be bedridden for days, judging by the depth of the slashes. He had to deal with this demon before it killed anyone else.

"*You will have to kill it,*" Rune said.

"*I can get it into the compass.*"

"*It has seen us. It will kill you to get to us.*"

"*And why is that?*" Quentin asked, suddenly suspicious. "*Why is this demon so hellbent on getting to you?*"

"*Please. Every demon we come across tries to kill us once they figure out why we're there. What makes this one so special?*"

"*Because it seems personal.*"

"*It's not.*"

Nothing about this demon made sense. Its victims were so random. Why here? Why now? And why these people? It was as though it had a purpose. Demons didn't usually have a purpose. They set up shop and fed off anyone they could. They rarely killed without reason. They were like rattlers that way. Except rattlers didn't feed off human souls. So, there was that.

After Amber had slipped the T-shirt over her head, Quentin turned to her and held up the jacket. The tee hung loosely over her shoulders and hips. The coat would swallow her, but she needed to stay warm. Shock was a strange and deadly thing.

"You need that more than I do," she said, refusing his offer.

"I really don't."

He shook the jacket, a khaki tactical, in front of her, and she slid her arms inside with a heavy sigh. When he turned her around and pulled it tight, he tried not to laugh. The sleeves were miles too long. He rolled up the right, waiting for her delicate fingers to show themselves, then the left. After zipping it up to just under her clavicle, he stepped back and took a look. The baggy jacket made her look like a kid. She was anything but.

"Better?" he signed.

She hugged herself and nodded.

"Then let's eat," he said, hungrier than ever. Only, no longer for food. He was such a perv.

Chapter Seven

She was such a perv. She couldn't stop glancing in Quentin's direction every few seconds. He walked like a predator, his gait smooth, his gaze ever watchful. What had he become? How had he transformed so much in just a few short years? And he was now a seasoned demon hunter? How did one become a seasoned demon hunter? How did one become a demon hunter at all? She hadn't even known that was a real thing.

After motioning for Dora and Kyle—who'd been standing off to one side, keeping watch—to join them, she followed Quentin to the Mine Shaft Tavern and Cantina. The minute they stepped into the cavernous place, a pretty redhead taking a large group's order seemed to recognize Quentin. She stopped and made a point to smile at him.

He probably gathered fans wherever he went. He'd always been gorgeous, but that attribute had somehow intensified tenfold. He was rigid and complex and confident, yet a sweetness lay just below his hard surface. She'd sensed it instantly. Wanted to drown in it. Missed it like she'd missed baklava that time she gave up sugar.

Then again, he'd almost crushed her larynx not thirty minutes ago. So, there was that.

She was a veteran of the supernatural realm, however. She knew enough about it to recognize that something had come over him. The question was, what? What had he gotten himself into?

They sat at a corner table. The place was brighter than she remembered, but it had been a while since she and her friends had visited the dusty, eclectic town. The Tavern bar had the same log-cabin feel, and the tables were the same heavy wood designed for the wear and tear of an active cantina. The local favorite was famous for several things, but their margaritas and green chile cheeseburgers were among the top.

Fortunately, the table they sat at had four chairs. She pulled out the two spare seats for Kyle and Dora, then took one that faced the bar. The place was getting busy already. Hopefully, no one would need one of their spares.

Clearly intimidated by He Who Turned into a Badass Demon Hunter Overnight, Kyle almost lunged for the chair beside Amber. Dora frowned at him and took the chair by the wall. Quentin had noticed. He sat across from Kyle and fixed him with a tormenting glare.

Kyle sank down in his seat, clutching his clipboard, and she chastised Quentin with an admonishing scowl. "Don't be a bully."

He turned the full force of his glare on her, his eyes glistening in the low light. It didn't have quite the same effect. Her stomach clenched and flip-flopped as molten lava pooled low in her abdomen, and she found herself struggling for air.

The server hurried over with two menus. She stopped short, her gaze bouncing from Kyle to Dora and back again before she came to her senses and refocused on Quentin. "Hello, again," she spoke and signed.

She was older than Quentin, though not by much. And she was pretty. Pretty enough to cause the sharp and utterly useless monster known as jealousy to rear its ugly head. Amber was not the jealous type. Normally. Then again, nothing about today had been normal.

"If you guys know what you want," the woman said quietly, "I'll put your order in before that large table."

"Green chile cheeseburger!" Amber blurted. "With sweet potato fries." She was suddenly starving. "You still have those, right?"

The woman smiled. "We do. What would you like to drink?"

"Just coffee, thanks." Though she craved one of their margaritas like there was no tomorrow.

The woman turned and beamed at Quentin. "And you?"

He had yet to take his eyes—and that glare—off Amber. "The same," he said softly.

"You got it, hon." The woman gave another furtive glance at their two guests and hurried off.

"She can see you guys," Amber said to them.

"That's Sarah." Dora looked at her as though she were a long-lost daughter, and Amber guessed that she did that a lot. "She's a darling girl. Been in town for a couple of months. Works breakfast at The Java Junction and lunch here at the Tavern. I hope she stays."

Recognition hadn't flashed across Sarah's face, so Amber guessed the server could *see* ghosts, for lack of a better word, but—like many eyewitness accounts—could only see them as a misty gray presence. Or even a slight shift in the shadows. Amber had never been able to see them until she died, and her aunt Charley had brought her back from the afterworld. When she woke up, she could suddenly see them in all their glory. And hear them. And play checkers with them, though she had to move the pieces for both players. Until Kyle came along, that is.

It was almost worth that horrible death.

Almost.

But enough about that. She glanced back at Quentin. "Okay, first things first," she said as they waited for their food. Then she realized that she had so many questions, she didn't know where to start.

A scythe-shaped brow inched up as Quentin waited for her interrogation.

"Right." She filled her lungs. Where to start? "Okay, how about you tell me how you became a demon hunter?"

He lifted a shoulder and signed, "I work for the Vatican."

She blinked, taking a moment to absorb that information. "The...*the* Vatican?"

"Yes."

"As in the pope? Smoke signals? The Sistine Chapel?"

"Yes. You know how the Vatican was watching us all back then?"

"I do." Amber's mother had told her. They'd mostly been watching her aunt Charley, what with her being part grim reaper and part god. And her uncle Reyes, aka the son of Satan and also a god. But they'd also been watching Amber. Probably because of the early signs of her clairvoyance. Admittedly, that fact freaked her out a little. If they knew how much her abilities had grown since then, they'd probably *still* be watching her. Then again, maybe they were. She would have no way of knowing.

"They recruited me when I was at Gallaudet," he signed.

"They recruited you?"

"Yes. Into a unit called La Guardia Segreta."

"The Secret Guard. They hunt demons?"

"Among other things. They mostly investigate supernatural events."

Sarah brought their coffee, slipped Quentin a flirtatious smile, then went to take the order of a man who'd taken the table next to them. He wore a Hawaiian shirt, a straw hat, and a long, gray ponytail—definitely a local.

"Okay," Amber said to Quentin. "Why you?"

He tipped his head to one side. "You would have to ask them."

"So, they recruited you, and you just up and left?"

He didn't answer. As usual. All she knew from back then was that Quentin had been found unconscious and was in the hospital. She and her mom had flown to DC that night, and she sat by his side for two days. When he woke, she knew. Something had changed. Something was different. He'd become a different person while at college.

A month later, he took his finals and was due home, when he sent her an email telling her that he wouldn't be on the flight. Nothing else. No explanation. No goodbye. No closure.

She'd tried calling. She was ashamed to say she'd called hundreds of times over the next few days. But he refused to answer, and eventually, shut off his phone. Amber was so devastated she almost didn't graduate high school. It took an intervention from both the living and the dead to get her back on track.

She ended up graduating a semester early and getting accepted into some of the best schools in the Southwest, but her heart was set on the East Coast for some reason. No, not for *some reason*. She knew why. *He* was on the East Coast. At least, she'd thought he was.

One weekend when she could no longer stand it, she'd hopped on a train in New York and went to DC, even though she knew that he was no longer there. She stumbled upon a couple of his friends at Gallaudet. He'd been gone for over a year at that point, but they remembered the event quite vividly. He was there one day and gone the next. He just packed up his things in the middle of the night and left without so much as a by your leave.

The pain of that time was still raw, even now. Amber and Quentin had been best friends for years. And then they were more. She'd given her heart to him. For him to just leave like that...

Obviously, there was more to the story, but why didn't he just tell her? She could've helped. He'd chosen not to tell her the truth, and he would have to live with that. She was nowhere near forgiving him. The fact that she craved him like an addict craved their next fix meant nothing.

Then again, it wasn't as if he'd asked for her forgiveness. He watched her from behind the depths of his shimmering blue eyes. Waited for her to reach whatever conclusion she was going to reach because he clearly wasn't going to explain himself.

The sting in her chest felt like an angry hornets' nest. She took a sip of coffee and then asked rather pettily, "Why are you signing? You speak perfectly well, Quentin. I've heard you."

"How about we get off of me and back to the business at hand?" he said. With his voice. Not his hands. He dropped the charade and refocused on Dora. "Why did that demon choose you?"

Surprised at becoming the center of attention, the woman blinked at him. "I have no idea.

"Dora, did the demon actually attack you?"

"Well…" She seemed to think for a bit. "I don't know. I mean, it was just there and…and then I fell. I'm just not sure."

Dora looked at Quentin. "That's odd, right? I mean, it didn't attack the first responders at the scene, either. In fact, the only one it has actually attacked is you. It doesn't like you."

Quentin turned to look out the window. "It doesn't like what's inside me."

Fighting to keep her cool—could he really be opening up?—Amber leaned forward. "What's inside you?"

The wary gaze he leveled on her spoke volumes. "Anger. Frustration. A thundering resentment I can hardly contain."

She sank back in her chair, disappointment chafing every molecule in her body. He didn't trust her.

"Why are we back on me when a demon is killing people?"

He had a point. "I just can't figure out why it's so volatile."

"Demon?" Quentin said, his voice dripping with sarcasm. At least, he'd mastered the language.

"No, there's more. I can't describe it. It's like…" She looked at him. "Well, it's like anger. Frustration. A thundering resentment he can hardly contain." Then it hit her. Control. The demon was being controlled by someone very much like Quentin was being controlled, at least in part, by the entity inside him. Only a loss of control would bring about that kind of resentment. That kind of bitterness. "You said you've been tracking the demon. How?"

"A variety of ways. I can track it to a degree with the compass." He took it out and showed it to her. "From there, I look for news stories and read police blotters. It always kills at least two people, often more, but never just one."

The round compass looked like an antique brass pillbox, but it was indeed a compass when Amber opened it. One that had seen better days. It was scratched and marred and beat up, much like its owner. Four tiny, amber jewels indicated the four directions: north, south, east, and west.

It emitted an otherworldly heat, but before she could examine it further, Quentin took it back and closed the lid.

"The Secret Guard gave that to you?"

"Not exactly. More like they allowed me to keep it. To help with my investigations."

"You mean, you found that?"

He hesitated, his face forming a thoughtful frown, and said, "In a way, yes. But I had help."

"And the dagger?"

"I had help finding that, too."

"But it'll kill the demon?"

"If I can get in a good swing, yes. I just need to eat." He was looking a little peaked, his pallor ghostly as though his strength were waning, and Amber straightened in her chair as alarm crept through her. "Are you okay?"

"I'm fine," he said, almost seeming annoyed that she'd asked. Asshat.

The entire time they spoke, Kyle had kept busy scribbling notes. It was what he did. Quentin glared at him, but Kyle missed it, he was so busy transcribing their conversation.

"Hey," she said to Quentin, her tone warning, "don't get mad at him. He's just doing his job."

"And what exactly does he do for you?"

The way he said it, as though he were jealous in some way, took her by surprise. She leaned forward and said, "He's done more for me than you ever did." That was a lie, but he didn't need to know that.

He bit down and looked at his watch, then toward the kitchen in annoyance. "I need to get back. Anyone with a key could open that front door now."

"That's bad?"

"I contained the demon inside the salt circle. If anyone opens that door, they'll break it, and the demon will escape."

"Crap. Hopefully, the police tape will keep the family out."

"My family," Dora said softly. "What they must be going through."

"I'm sorry, hon."

She clasped her hands together and averted her gaze.

Kyle stopped scribbling and looked at her, his expression anxious. "Ms. Kowalski, I hate to bring this up, but you have an appointment at two."

Amber pressed her palms to her eyes and then scrubbed her face. "Crap. Mrs. Harmon." There went two hundred bucks she really could've used. And if she didn't get ahold of the woman to reschedule, she could lose her business for good. Yet, a demon was holding her phone hostage.

"Mrs. Harmon?" Quentin asked.

"Her best client," Kyle said and then snorted. "Woman's crazy." When Quentin merely glared at him, Kyle cleared his throat and went back to taking notes.

What the actual hell? What did he have against Kyle?

But Dora leaned in, intrigued. "You're investigating something for her?"

Amber shook her head. "Not exactly. I read her cards. It's what I do. Kind of. Like an on-the-side thing."

"Really? Can you read mine?" she asked, her eyes bright with fascination.

"I don't... I mean, I've never tried to read the cards for a departed." But the more she thought about it, the more it made sense. "Let's give it a shot. Maybe something will come up that'll explain all of this."

Dora gasped in excitement and squirmed in her chair, but Amber remembered one pertinent detail: Her cards were with her phone, which was in her purse, which was in Dora's house, which was currently occupied by a bloodthirsty demon. Still, it wasn't like she used real tarot cards anyway. The cards she used were completely blank. Black on one side, white on the other. She didn't actually read them. She used them as a tool to *dive*, as she called it. To delve into the person's life. Into their psyche. Their past and present and future. But she did need something. It was more in the movement, the flipping of the cards.

She looked around. The napkins weren't quite right, but the

coasters... "Perfect." She gathered the four coasters on the table, the round ones with *The Mine Shaft Cantina* written on them. The backs were blank, a dark brown. They would work, but she might need... She leaned over and asked Hawaii if she could borrow his.

He lifted a shoulder, so she scooped them up and straightened in her chair, all under the watchful gaze of Quentin Rutherford. And now, Hawaii, who was suddenly very interested, though he pretended not to be.

That was okay. The fact that she would have to talk to air? Oh, well. She'd looked mad before. She should fit right in here.

Dora was on her right. "Okay, just concentrate on me. I'm not sure if I can do this, but I'll try."

"Gotcha. Concentrate. I am so there."

She tapped the coasters, seven in total, straightening them in her hands and then focusing on Dora. She really was a lovely woman. Short and curvy, she looked younger than her age, which she'd confessed during their initial interview was a surprising fifty-five.

She drew in a deep breath and relaxed. Or she tried to. It was harder than she thought it would be, thanks to her audience. Not Hawaii. Quentin. The blistering, scruffy sexpot keeping a close eye on everything she did.

Then again, maybe it was the town. The mystical merry-go-round called Madrid, emphasis on the *Mad*. Maybe its energies were short-circuiting hers.

She wiggled her shoulders and tried again, shaking off any negativity—like, say, the kind radiating from the delicacy sitting across from her. Concentrating on Dora's kind eyes, Amber focused on her goal to help the woman. To help everyone in the town. Who knew who could be next if the demon escaped? But the question popped into her head again. Why these three people? In this town? There had to be a connection. Something must have lured the demon to them.

Amber put the coasters in her left hand, printed side up, and slid the top one to the side with her thumb, all while pushing out any and all emotion. She then took the coaster in her right hand and flipped it. The movement caused a slight breeze on the air, like a butterfly's wings, and the familiar action stopped time. At least, in her head. Everything around her faded away as she put the coaster on the table in front of her client. Her lids became heavy. The noise of the tavern sounded like it was underwater. And she saw through Dora's eyes.

Knowing time was pressing, she searched quickly. Dora's memories were lovely. She'd had a good life. Lots of friends and a family who truly cared for each other. But three events stood out. Three tragedies.

The first was a car accident when she was a little girl. The one in which she'd lost her beloved father. She remembered it. The screeching of the tires. The loud, solid crash as another car T-boned them. The glass spraying across her face and arms.

There was simply life before and life after. It divided her existence into two separate parts and took a year for her to be able to get into a car again.

But that didn't explain why a demon had shown up, wanting a piece of her. Amber moved past that traumatic memory to the next. She'd been robbed at gunpoint in Dallas outside a pub. She'd handed the guy in a ski mask her clutch. Then he wanted her necklace—the one her father had given her two days before the crash. She'd told him no, so he clocked her with the butt of the gun and ripped it off her neck anyway. It had taken two surgeries to fix her orbital socket and two years to get her necklace back. She'd hired a PI. It was worth every penny.

But, again, nothing to explain the demon. Unfortunately, the third event didn't explain much either. Dora was a bus driver and had been taking her last and youngest student home—a first-grader named Madeline. She lived in a compound off the grid with a few families several miles outside of Madrid. The mobile homes were ancient, the campers dilapidated and lopsided.

Dora had pulled down the dusty road and found that the cattle guard had collapsed. She couldn't cross it, but the houses were barely a quarter of a mile up the road. So, she'd dropped off the girl and watched to make sure she walked all the way into the compound—not that she had anywhere else to go.

That night, the cops came to Dora's house. Madeline had never made it home.

It was her worst nightmare. The entire town spent days trying to find the girl. They scoured the desert countryside, searched every structure in the compound, put bulletins all over the town, Santa Fe, and Albuquerque. The local police, state police, and the FBI questioned Dora repeatedly. She'd watched Madeline walk over the hill to the commons area of the compound. Something had to have happened afterward, but nobody saw anything. They didn't even see her go into the home she shared with her mother, which was little more than a camper shell. The girl was never seen again. And while utterly heartbreaking, it *still* didn't explain the demon.

Maybe she could get back to that someday. Help Dora get closure. But for now, they had to focus on the danger at hand.

Disappointment spread through Amber like acid. She didn't know what she'd expected to find. A clue. A hint of something supernatural happening to Dora that might link back to this. But there was simply nothing.

She could see Quentin watching her through her periphery. His head tilted to one side. His eyes shimmered. His hand rested on the table, one finger tapping as though in slow motion. She didn't even try to see into Dora's future. She didn't know if she could with Dora being in the afterworld. So, she decided to take advantage of the situation in front of her.

She took another coaster and timed its flip perfectly. She shifted her gaze to Quentin's, flipped the card, and laid it in front of him a millisecond before he realized what she was doing. He started to get up, to stop her, but it was too late. She dove inside him.

Or more like fell.

Shapes hit her first. Lots of movement and shadows, like a colony of bugs in the dark. An entire dimension, scurrying and smoky and blue. And then the eyes came into focus. The black eyes. Hundreds of them. Thousands.

"Rune," she whispered. Quentin didn't have a demon inside him. He had hundreds of thousands. He had an entire dimension. A dimension named Rune.

Chapter Eight

I try to act nonchalant,
but underneath, I'm chalant as fuck.
—T-shirt

"You shouldn't be here, Traveler."

One of them spoke to her—or maybe all of them—and the surprise that shot through Amber almost knocked her out of the dive, but she had fallen inside and didn't know how to get out. She searched frantically but couldn't find an exit, so she faced them. Hordes. As far as the eye could see.

"What did you do to him?" she asked, her voice a mere hiss. And yet, she hadn't spoken. Not out loud.

"We sought refuge, Traveler. The one named Quinn gave it."

"That's not his name."

"It is, and you know it."

She did. That was his birth name. But how did *they* know that when even Quentin didn't? She'd researched for years and found his birth parents.

"You do not know what he did for us."

She raised her chin. Metaphorically. *"Then tell me."*

"How about I show you?"

Before she could agree or disagree, the smoke and shadows parted, and memories rushed past her so fast, she could hardly keep up. Running. Fighting. Inhuman screaming. And then everything went silent. They had jumped into another dimension. One they called the House of the Founding Fathers. Washington DC. They lived there for centuries, but they were starving. Buildings rose and fell around them.

Humans lived and died.

And then his face. He was different. Born of this world but from another. Quentin, only not. He absorbed them, not the other way around. He took them into his breast. Sheltered them. But it'd almost killed him. He ended up in the hospital. Rune remembered Amber being there, but those early days were disorienting. They could not see clearly. But they were nourished. For the first time in centuries, they were no longer starving.

Once Quentin was better, they returned to his school with him, but he started suspecting that they were there. He felt them. A twitch. A rustle. Until one day, he was out with his friends and heard one of them speak. He could talk better than the others, and Quentin heard him. He'd thought he was going crazy. Why could he suddenly hear?

"He's hearing through you," Amber said to them, astonished.

"Yes. But there is more, Traveler. Pay attention."

She started to chastise them—she did not like being told what to do—but they showed her the nightmares that would leave him sweating and disoriented until he saw her face and calmed. He only wanted to get back to her. To finish out the semester and go home.

He'd already decided not to return to Gallaudet. He would go wherever she was. He would get a job. Take classes at night with an interpreter. Whatever it took to be with her. But, somehow, they found out about him. *La Guardia Segreta.* They came like thieves in the night.

Amber gasped as Rune showed her what they did to him. They knew he was possessed. They just had no clue that there was more than one entity inside him. Even Quentin didn't know it at the time. They flew him halfway across the world and took him to an underground lab. It looked like a basement with both ancient and modern forms of technology. They tried to get the demon out. They wanted it alive. They wanted to study it.

A doctor named Tinari headed the project, and he was willing to kill Quentin to get to the demon. But then he discovered Quentin's healing ability, and Tinari decided he wanted to study that, too. He and his team pushed Quentin to his physical and mental limits. How much pain could he take? How fast could he heal from a bullet wound?

Amber closed her eyes, but she could still see. The beatings. The starvation. The constant torture. All in the name of science.

After several weeks, they finally extracted a demon. Quentin and Rune were both dying and, in their weakened states, the men working on them were able to extract one of the entities with a compass similar to the one Quentin carried. But something went wrong. The extraction killed the massive beast. It died almost instantly and crumbled to dust.

That was when Quentin had had enough. He broke the metal cuffs securing him to a stainless surgical chair and killed every person in the room in a matter of seconds—five total. He saved the doctor for last. The one who'd tried to run but was so scared that he couldn't get the code right on the keypad.

Alarms blared and lights flashed as Quentin towered behind the doctor. Quentin reached around the quivering man and said, "Here, let me help you." After typing in the code, he stood back.

The door opened, and Tinari gaped up at him, his eyes like saucers. He started to make a run for it when Quentin grabbed him from behind and snapped his neck. The man crumpled to the floor, and Quentin looked at him for a long moment before glancing up and seeing his reflection in a stainless-steel paper towel dispenser.

His eyes were solid black like wet ink. His hair, tangled and unkempt, hung in patches, and he had the beginnings of a sparse beard over a purple, swollen jaw. His lips were cracked and bleeding, and his nose had been broken numerous times.

He didn't recognize himself. Amber didn't recognize him either, and she almost blacked out from the pain the image caused.

Quentin grabbed a handful of the demon's dust and sat back on the chair they had tortured him in for weeks as though it were his throne. He curled the dust into his fist and held it to his mouth as tears slipped past his lashes.

A small army dressed in full tactical gear filed into the room. The guards pointed their entire armory at him. Thirty guns aimed right at his head as he waited. And grieved. Finally, three men in suits came in. The guards parted for them but kept their aim steady. The men looked around, and the one who was clearly in charge, a fair-haired man who spoke with an Italian accent, said three words to Quentin: "*Name your price.*"

And from that moment on, Quentin worked for the very men who had kidnapped and tortured him, but he got to keep Rune safe. And Amber. He got to keep Amber safe because if Rune could take over in the span of a heartbeat and kill so mercilessly, he could not risk her life by going to her. At the same time, he would not be responsible for the deaths of hundreds of thousands of innocent entities who had never harmed a human in their lives.

Until now.

Amber felt tears on her face and didn't know if it was real or not. On this plane or hers. The sadness emanating from Rune—or the single entity talking to her—stole her breath. "*You knew the one they killed.*"

After a long moment, he answered. "*My son.*"

More tears slipped past her lashes. "*I'm so sorry.*"

"*You call us demons. We call you monsters.*"

She nodded. "*That's fair.*"

"*That's fear. Nothing more. We are sorry we almost killed you earlier.*"

She shook her head. "*Did you?*"

"*Your throat. We took over. Quentin was bleeding to death. We had to stop it.*"

"*Then I'm grateful.*" She looked out at the sea of faces. Yes, they were the stuff of nightmares with razor-sharp teeth and large, glistening eyes, but they didn't want to kill her any more than she wanted to kill them. "*Rune, do you know anything about this demon he's been tracking? What it wants?*"

"*Besides us? No.*"

"*You?*"

"*It is starving. It could live for centuries off our essence. And now it has seen us. It will kill Quentin to feed.*"

"*That's why he was attacked.*"

"*Yes. Please don't worry, Traveler. We will relinquish our lives before that happens.*"

"*What? No. Rune, we'll figure something out.*"

"*Perhaps. But we will not let Quentin die for us. He has done so much already.*"

She thought about it. If she could talk to this entity like she was talking to Rune, maybe... "*Rune, can you keep Quentin here for a little while? Like, under your thrall?*"

"*I can, but he will not be happy about it.*"

"*Good. Let him sulk.*"

"*Traveler, have you ever heard of a demon hunter sulking?*"

"*No.*"

"*That's because no one has ever caused one to sulk and lived to tell the tale.*"

She laughed and mentally lowered her head. "*Thank you, Rune, for saving his life.*"

"*And almost taking yours in the process? Any time, Traveler. Be careful. This demon is furious.*"

"*Yes, I could tell.*" Amber didn't know if she rose out of the dive of her own volition or if Rune had released her, but suddenly she was back at the Tavern.

"Are you getting anything?" Dora asked.

Amber blinked and glanced around, waiting for her pupils to adjust. Quentin was staring at her, but his eyes were pitch-black. "Son of a bitch." She patted the jacket and felt the sunglasses she'd found in a pocket earlier. She unfolded them and pushed them onto Quentin's handsome face—the one that had taken so much abuse—then she looked at Dora. "How long was I out?"

"Out? What do you mean? You just flipped over two coasters." She sat back in disappointment. "You're not getting anything, are you?"

"Oh, I got tons. Did I ever. If Quentin comes to, tell him I went to the bathroom."

Kyle panicked and stood when she did. "Wait, where are you going?"

"To the bathroom. That way, you won't have to lie. I'm just going to do it at Dora's house."

"Oh, good heavens." Dora covered her eyes like that would somehow stop Amber from leaving.

Amber laughed softly and then remembered what she was about to do. This could be the biggest mistake of her life. And her last chance to do something she'd been wanting to do since that morning. Risking Quentin coming to, she cupped his scruffy jaw, bent over, and brushed her mouth across his. He was warm and slightly feverish, a fact that spurred her into action.

Sarah brought their food just as Amber grabbed the coasters and turned to leave. "Wonderful, I'll be right back. Don't take my plate away. Oh, and Quentin is taking a quick power nap. But really," she said as she rushed out, "don't take my plate. I'll just be a minute."

She tore out of the Tavern and ran all the way to Dora's house, gasping for air when she got there. She went around to the back door to find Kyle blocking it. Literally. He held his arms across the doorframe, clipboard in one hand and pen in the other. "I can't let you do this, Ms. Kowalski. If anything happens to you, I'll be out of a job."

"Your concern is touching, Kyle," she said between gasps. "And it's not like I pay you."

"But you do. In other ways." He pushed his round glasses up his nose then returned his hand to the frame.

"Kyle, look… Wait, what ways? Have you seen me naked?"

He bit his bottom lip and shook his head.

What the hell? "Never mind. You realize I can just walk through you?"

"Yes, I do. But that's rude, and you would never…"

She walked through him and opened the back door. Kyle gaped at her, appalled.

"Sorry, Charlie. I'm on a mission."

"You're going to get killed."

She narrowed her eyes and looked up toward the attic window. "I don't think so."

"And how many demons have you befriended lately?"

The grin that crept across her face could not be helped. "Hundreds of thousands."

He scoffed, then said, "Wait, really?" before dropping his ghost clipboard. It didn't make a sound.

Amber stepped into the house, careful to stay inside the black salt lines. She walked to the center of the small kitchen. Having no idea how long she had, how long Rune could hold Quentin, she drew in a deep breath and stepped out of the circle. Then she closed her eyes and waited.

Her hands shook at her sides, and she almost dropped the coasters. She'd been killed by something from the afterworld once already. She did not care for a repeat performance. When she was still breathing twenty seconds later, and her innards were still…innardly as opposed to outerly, she took a reluctant step toward the stairs. That was when she heard it. The breathing. The raspy inhales and exhales of an injured animal.

Swallowing hard, she started up the stairs, taking them slowly to let the demon know she was not a threat. Then again, it'd killed at least three people—more if Quentin was correct—and as far as anyone knew, it hadn't actually touched any of them. It could crush her skull with a collectible rattlesnake paperweight or decapitate her with one of the vintage New Mexico license plates hanging on the walls. Any number of gruesome deaths awaited her.

When she got to the top floor, she looked around. The rasps were coming from the same corner the demon had occupied before, hidden by shelves of supplies and inventory.

She sat on the floor, crossed her legs, and took the coasters into both hands. Maybe she could communicate with it, try to understand why it was here, but she couldn't dive if she couldn't see into its eyes. Or could she?

Closing her eyes again, she concentrated on its breathing. She could feel its energies in the room—heavy and full of static. It sent electrical currents flickering over her skin.

She focused on that. Its energy. Its breathing. Its presence. Then she flipped a coaster and laid it on the floor as time slowed around her. The air thickened, and her shoulders relaxed.

Its anger washed over her first. Its rage. She let it. Absorbed it and tried to understand it. Why? Why these victims? Why here? Why now? A clicking sounded in the distance, like someone typing on a keyboard. And then faces flashed in her mind like the flickering of a silent film. A rotund businessman in Chicago. A beloved grandfather in Seattle. A pretty senator in Kentucky. Face after face of people it had killed. But it always killed *the other*, as well. It called its last victims at any given place *the other*, and part of a face she recognized flashed on the screen of her mind's eye.

A gravelly voice registered nearby. It said three syllables as though they were foreign on its tongue. As though it were only just learning to say them. "Tra…vel…er."

Her eyes flew open to find the demon inches from her face. She jumped and scrambled back, her gaze darting toward the stairs. But it was so fast. She didn't think for a minute she could make it down the stairs and into the circle before it caught up to her.

"Tra…vel…er," it repeated. Its voice was just as raspy as its breathing. Its eyes almost completely black except for a horizontal green line that ran straight across them. What evolution had in mind there, she had no idea.

It stepped closer and hooked a massive claw over her ankle to hold her in place. She fell back and tried to pull her foot free as it straddled her, bent, and sniffed. It smelled her hair and her face and her neck where its forked tongue slithered out for a taste, and Amber felt the world tumble beneath her.

The demon was an odd pattern of grays and blacks with gold splattered about, and smooth, shell-shaped scales covered its body. It looked similar to the entities in Rune but more reptilian.

It spoke again, slowly, struggling to pronounce the words through its long, needlelike teeth. "What are you doing?"

"I... I'm trying to find out what you want."

Roughly the size of a rhinoceros and only partially solid—it would not fit in the room, otherwise—it was hunched, slender, and agile. Able to solidify parts of its body at any given time, it took a massive claw and ripped her jacket open at the stomach as the blood drained from her face.

This was it. This was officially the stupidest thing she'd ever done.

The demon focused on her stomach. Bringing its other talon around, it sank a claw into the T-shirt and split it in two. Then it sniffed some more. Nudged. Licked the sensitive skin as Amber fought the darkening of her vision.

"Freedom," it said, its deep voice like rocks being crushed. "And food." It threaded his teeth into the front of the jacket and pulled her into a sitting position. She almost blacked out when it added, "Not necessarily in that order."

It started to walk around her, sniffing her hair and nudging her back.

She decided to negotiate. "We can help each other."

"Doubt it, Tra-vel-er."

Why did everyone keep calling her *Traveler*? Was that another word for clairvoyant or something?

"Set me free," it said at her ear. Its tongue slithered out and curled around her jaw for a taste. "I seek the summoner."

"I'm afraid I can't do that," she said, her voice more air than sound.

It growled so loud, the rafters shook, and Amber realized she should have done what she said she was going to do. She should have gone to the bathroom.

A container above her shook off a shelf and crashed beside her, spraying an industrial cleaner over her pants, but a couple of drops flew into her eyes. She rubbed them, making them burn even more. Shaking visibly now, she forced herself to stay still. She had seen what those teeth were capable of. Those claws. What they had done to Quentin in the blink of an eye. She didn't move. Didn't dare give it a reason to attack. But it was certainly capable of rational thought. She could work with that, right?

When it stopped growling, she gathered her courage and asked softly, "Are you finished?"

It completed its inspection and faced her again. "Just getting started."

She had been afraid of that. Its mouth peeled back, and its teeth elongated, extending another two inches. "Free me," it said, as though giving her one last chance a microsecond before she saw movement out of the corner of her eye.

The demon screamed and flew back to its corner as black salt hit it.

Amber closed her eyes and covered her face against the assault, only to feel herself being lifted off the floor. Quentin pulled her up, and she hugged him, literally wrapping both her arms and legs around him and holding on for dear life.

They sailed over the stairs, landed in the hall, and were out the back door before she could even fill her lungs to scream. By the time she did, it was far too late. And more than a little awkward.

Chapter Nine

This killing them with kindness
is taking way longer than expected.
—Meme

He didn't stop. While she kept the death grip tight, trying to remain conscious, Quentin carried her all the way to his truck, where he opened the back door and set her on the seat. But she was still clinging on for dear life.

He let her. For a few minutes. He buried his face in her hair and hugged her back just as hard. Then, as though coming to his senses, he shoved her away from him and pointed to the duffle bag. His eyes were solid black, but the color was shrinking into inky tendrils, the depths of his cobalt irises now showing through. "There are clothes in there. You'll have to dig through it to find the sweats. They have a drawstring so they should be okay."

She looked down. The cleaner had soaked through her pants, the smell pungent and acrid. And Quentin's shirt had a wet spot where she'd tried to fuse their molecules together. But the jacket and shirt hung open, exposing part of her bra. She scrambled back and tried to cover her embarrassment with the ripped coat.

A jacket he had yet to notice. The moment his gaze dropped to the gaping hole in what hopefully was not his favorite fashion statement, his eyes began to blacken again, just barely, the reaction clearly controlled by emotion. He pulled her closer again and tore it open. Looking for any injuries. Sliding his hand over her stomach and her rib cage and her—

"I'm okay," she said, pushing at his hands and trying to close the jacket. Her cheeks were wet and now burned with embarrassment. And industrial cleaner. And black salt. She could only imagine what they looked like.

He took her by the arms and asked, "Why the fuck would you do that?"

She hiccupped before answering. "I was trying to find out what it wanted."

He jerked her closer until their faces were centimeters apart. His was the picture of rage when he asked, "Why the fuck would you have Rune hold me like that?"

She tried to squirm out of his grasp. She failed. "You… You heard me?"

"I heard you." He jerked again, but he did it in such a way as to not hurt her. It was more for show. His muscles and tendons corded with the effort, an effort she imagined was born more out of his desire not to hurt her than vice versa. "I heard everything. I just couldn't do anything about it." His jaw clenched in anger, he let her go as though disgusted with her. "You had no right to do that."

"I know." She had violated him. Entered his mind without permission. She'd vowed never to do that years ago and now… He had every reason to be livid. Then again, so did she. "I get it. I had no right. But you had no right not to tell me what happened to you. Not after everything we'd been through. You just left." Her voice cracked, and she turned to go through the duffle bag. She found a T-shirt and a pair of gray sweats with a drawstring and started stripping. "*You* left *me*." She lifted the torn T-shirt over her head, suddenly uncaring of what he saw and what he didn't. Clearly, she disgusted him. She fought the trembling of her traitorous lower lip as she slipped on his T-shirt. It was tan with the words *Blue Sun* on it and Chinese characters underneath. "They took you, yes, and I can't even imagine what you went through, but you decided to write me off without even talking to me." She kicked off her boots. "Without an explanation. Without even saying goodbye." She peeled her panties and leggings down over her hips and kicked them off. Her skin had pinkened where the cleaner had soaked through.

She wasn't worried about flashing anyone. His windows were so dark, an onlooker would literally have to press their face to the glass to see inside. It was dark and cool and safe.

He got into the truck and closed the door, forcing her to scoot over. But he had crap everywhere. A medical kit. A crossbow. Books, file folders, and a laptop. She shifted some of the items onto the floorboard as he grabbed the duffle bag, looking for another shirt since the cleaner had soaked through his shirt, too.

"You decided not to tell me anything. You were just…gone."

"It was best for everyone."

She turned on him, furious. "No, Quentin. It was best for you." She found a pre-moistened wipe in the first-aid kit and ripped it open with her teeth. "We'd been best friends for years, and then *bam.* You just left. The country, as it turned out. So, you can absolutely kiss my ass."

Apparently not finding the shirt he was looking for, he shoved the duffle bag into the front seat and sat back. He put an elbow on the armrest and a fist at his mouth as he looked out the window, the blue of his irises glistening in the New Mexico sun. "I didn't want you to see any of that."

She wiped down her stomach and lower extremities then stopped to look at him. He had to change his shirt and possibly the bandages. Industrial cleaners on open wounds could not be good.

"We need to check your injuries." She slipped a leg into the sweats. "Did carrying me rip anything open?"

He shook his head as she slid the other leg in and then leaned back to lift her hips off the seat and pull the sweats on. They were far too big. The drawstring would help, but it had a knot she couldn't get untied, so she couldn't pull it tighter.

"I didn't want you to see me there. Like that." The muscle in his jaw jumped as he worked it. "Rune had no right to show you."

"If it's any consolation, I'm not sure Rune had a choice." And she wasn't. Her powers of persuasion were pretty persuasive. Drawing the string tighter so the sweats would hopefully not fall, even though she couldn't tie it, she got onto her knees and started lifting his shirt over his head. He reared back and looked at her as if she were crazy. "We need to check your bandages. Don't worry. You can still be mad at me." She tugged the T-shirt over his head, mussing his hair even more. Multiplying his adorable factor tenfold. Damn it.

He looked down and ran a hand over the gauze. "See? It didn't even soak through."

She sat back on her heels, now recognizing some of the scars. The heartbreaking images Rune had shown her flashed in her mind as she remembered where each scar originated. A line across his chest was from a scalpel. A small circle in his shoulder was from a bullet wound. A patch of marred skin was from an acid burn, though that one was kind of his fault.

But it was the scars on his wrists that stole her breath. She lifted his right wrist to her mouth and kissed the inside where the scars were. From when he had tried to take his life just to get it all to stop. Rune had healed him. Over and over again. She took the left one and did the same, shattering when she thought about what he had gone through. Then she ran her fingers along some of the other marks as the stinging in her eyes sent a fat drop spilling over her lashes.

He stilled and watched her with a wary gaze. "You don't have to feel sorry for me," he said, and she marveled again at how well he spoke. At how much she'd missed him. At how much she still wanted him desperately, despite everything. That demon could've killed her, and Quentin would've never known what he'd meant to her. What he still meant.

She leaned forward and brushed her mouth over a razor-thin scar on his shoulder. Then one on his neck. Then up to the cut on his cheek, feathering a soft kiss along his sculpted jaw.

He clutched the armrest with one hand and kept the other clenched at his side as though afraid to move.

Amber tried to remember that she disgusted him. She tried to remember that she hadn't been worthy of even a salty goodbye. And that he probably didn't enjoy her ministrations. But her memory seemed to be on the fritz.

She leaned back and looked at him. His handsome face, still so young and yet hardened. His full mouth framed by scruffy, dark-blond growth. His broad shoulders on which the weight of the world sat. He was so stunningly handsome. So painfully beautiful.

"You have to stop me," she said, running her hand over a wide shoulder and along the hills and valleys of his biceps. Lean and muscular, he was part human, part predator.

Poor guy had almost died less than an hour ago, and she was trying to have her way with him. If he'd wanted her, wouldn't he have made the first move? Perhaps, but he owed her the words. He owed her closure.

"Tell me you don't want me." Her hand slid over his bandages, caressing his rib cage and down to the waistband of his jeans. Despite the strong scent of industrial cleaner in the truck, she could smell him. His soap. She leaned forward to breathe in the woodsy scent, rich and warm like him. "Tell me you left me for a reason," she said into his ear.

She lowered her head to study the button and the zipper. The only two things standing between her and what she wanted most. "Tell me you don't love me." She pushed her fingertips into his jeans and released the button. "You never did." She slid the zipper down. "You've been happier without me." She pulled the two edges of his jeans apart, and the muscles in his abdomen contracted. "We will never work." She plunged her hand inside and wrapped her fingers around his erection as he sucked in a sharp breath. "It was never meant to be." She looked up at him and pleaded. "Just stop me already."

Black tendrils of ink had slid across his eyes as he watched her. Glistening and dark and dangerous, the blackness took over, but it was still him. She could see him in his expression. In the youthful lines of his face.

She tightened her hold. He bit down on his lip and released a soft groan before grabbing her wrist. But it was too late. She sank onto the floorboard between his legs, pulled him free, and slid her mouth over his steely cock.

He grabbed handfuls of hair to rein her in. She inched farther down anyway.

"Amber, fuck."

Reveling in her power over him, she eased back and then swallowed him again. He grabbed the armrest as she repeated her performance. She felt the blood rush through his rigid cock.

"Amber," he whispered a microsecond before he dragged her onto his lap and kissed her. His mouth was warm and heady, his scruff soft against her cheeks as he drove his tongue inside her mouth. Seeking. Tasting. Sucking. The kiss grew more desperate, nearly brutal in its exquisiteness.

Now straddling him, she wrapped her arms around his neck, broke off the kiss, and held his head to her breast. He moved his hand into the sweats and over her ass. One hand slid between her ass cheeks and between her legs. She squirmed, but he held her tight. Parted her folds. Dipped his fingers to wet them, then found her clit and circled it, his touch feathery soft, such a contrast to the rest of him.

The orgasm she'd been craving at his hands sparked to life beneath his deft touch, the pressure delicious. "Quentin," she said, burying her fingers in his hair.

He continued circling, his movements slow and meticulous.

She threw back her head and spread her knees farther apart to give him better access. To let the heat simmering in her abdomen come to a boil. With his free hand, he tugged at her shirt. She lifted it over her head, and he made quick work of her bra.

The cool air tightened her skin. He pulled her against him and took a nipple into his mouth. It sent heat flares to that place in her core where all the orgasms lived, waiting for their turn to blossom. She plucked one and coaxed it forward as his touch grew more urgent. As his tongue teased the delicate peak it had been nurturing.

His desire impatient, he lowered her onto the bench seat. He peeled the sweats off her and kissed the inside of her left ankle before perching that foot on the passenger's seat headrest. He kissed the inside of her right ankle and perched that foot on the back headrest, then continued peppering the inside of her leg with kisses, leaving heat trails on her skin. When his mouth sought her core and covered her clit, she almost came off the seat.

He forced her back down and suckled her clit softly as she writhed beneath him. She buried her hands in his hair as the world spiraled around her. "Quentin," she said, her voice more desperate than she'd planned. "Hurry."

He rose, ripped open a condom, and slid it over his rock-hard erection. She watched, her mouth watering as he stroked his cock, priming it for what came next. Then he hovered over her, his eyes solid black like a predator readying to devour its prey.

When he pressed into her, she dug her nails into his shoulders. It had been a very long time, but the pain only pushed her to greater heights. She fought for air as he slid inside her, burying himself in one long thrust. A movement that elicited a gasp before she remembered that he could hear her. Still, she gasped again when he slid out and plunged back inside.

His muscles had solidified. He reached one arm over and grabbed the door above his head, his hand, hard and masculine, starting to shake. A beautiful, dark kind of agony overcame him as he grew closer to climax.

She could hardly take her eyes off him, but her orgasm was skyrocketing toward her. She clutched him to her and locked both her arms and her legs around him as he drove into her, each thrust feeding the pressure building in her core. He pounded faster and faster, and she cried out when heat bloomed inside her like a nuclear reactor. It exploded, soaring through every molecule in her body, spilling over in sweet and stinging waves of pleasure.

"Holy fuck," he growled, pushing inside her and holding his position as his orgasm spasmed through his body. He ground his teeth and waited it out before easing his hold with a final, shuddering breath.

She grabbed handfuls of his hair and pulled him down to her, their quick breaths matching pace. Their heartbeats synchronizing.

When he rose and looked at her, his eyes were blue again. Unreal. Amazing, astonishing, magnificent, and unreal. And here she'd wanted to sleep in.

Chapter Ten

Large freight only.
—Women's underwear

She lay sprawled on top of Quentin on the backseat, marveling at the way the day had gone and the number of times she'd climaxed—mostly at the number of times she'd climaxed—when something the demon said hit her.

Again, it all boiled down to control. Quentin had been livid about the fact that Rune had taken control. That she'd had him take control. He'd lost the one thing he cherished most. His independence. His autonomy.

The demon wanted to be set free from the house. It wanted the salt line broken so it could leave. But it'd first said it wanted its freedom. What if it had been talking about two separate things? Even though it had completed its tasks, it'd still been in town. Waiting. The image of the woman Amber had seen popped into her head.

"Quentin, I think I know what's going on. Why the killings are so unusual for a demon. And so random."

He ran a hand lazily over her back. "I'm all ears."

"What if the demon has no free will? What if someone, or a group of someones, is controlling it? It told me it wanted its freedom and that it seeks the summoner. What if it meant freedom from the people controlling it? From the people *summoning* it?"

"What makes you think multiple people are controlling it?"

She rose and rested her chin on the back of her hands. "Remember how it kills at least two people everywhere it goes?"

"Hard to forget."

"And are those people always connected somehow?"

"Yes. It's one way I know it's the right demon. Strange deaths of two or more connected people that are unusual and days apart."

"I think it's killing the person it was summoned to kill and then killing the summoner as a way to gain its freedom. It wants control over its destiny, but people keep summoning it. When I read the demon, I got a lot of anger. A ton of frustration. Like it had no control, and that pissed it off. And," she said, stopping to chew on her lower lip a moment, "I know who it wants to kill next."

He stilled, clearly surprised. "You saw?"

She nodded. "I did." She looked toward the Tavern. "Sarah. I think she summoned it. It was weird. I heard clicking on a keyboard. Saw her face. It's something online. Some kind of chat room. Or cult."

"Same difference. The dark web has a lot of stuff like that."

"Yes. Exactly." Amber looked at him. "Quentin, I think Sarah wanted those three specific people dead for a reason, I just don't know why."

He lifted a shoulder. "Let's ask."

The fact that he believed her without question meant everything to her. He put his hand on the door handle, but she stopped him by reaching over and putting her hand over his.

When he questioned her with a gorgeously raised brow, she said, "In case something happens, in case this thing goes wrong, there's something you need to know."

He sat back, looking wary now. "Okay."

"I… I found your birth parents."

If she had told him that she was captaining the first manned mission to Mars, he likely would've been less surprised. He stilled completely. His full lips parted as he gazed at her. Then he shook his head. "That's impossible. I've—"

"You were right. You were born in DC. Your mother died when you were young. Your father raised you and…he's like you, Quentin." She put a hand on his shoulder. "He's Deaf, and he can see the departed just as clearly as you can."

"Can?" he asked in disbelief.

"Yes, can." A knowing grin spread across her face. "He's still in DC. He works at a cemetery digging graves and doing maintenance. I think he likes it there. I think it's peaceful for him. I didn't tell him I knew you. I wanted you to make that decision. But, Quentin, he's kind of wonderful."

"I don't understand. What happened? How did I end up——?"

"The first demon possession."

"Seems to be a theme with me, doesn't it?" True, but the first one was an entirely different breed of demon. Or maybe Rune was. Demons were not generally so family oriented. They were evil. Pure and simple.

"There aren't many people like you, apparently. From what I can gather, the demon that possessed you and sent you after my aunt Charley did so while you were on a school trip for football. You were the quarterback, by the way."

He shook his head, unable to remember any of his past.

"The demon took absolute control." Which would explain Quentin's fear of losing it. His anger at having lost it at her hands. "He had you send texts to your dad, telling him you were leaving. You'd had a fight, so it wasn't a huge surprise, but your dad feared you getting into trouble, so he didn't report you missing. He kept in touch. Begged you to come home. Quentin, the demon said some pretty nasty things to him. He never knew it wasn't you. A month later, Aunt Charley found you, and the rest is history."

He turned to look out the window.

Amber could tell how stunned he was. How hurt. She took his hand in hers. "Your real name is Quinn. Quinn Rutherford. So, you almost remembered it right. The demon didn't erase everything."

He rubbed his mouth, unable to believe what she was telling him. After all this time.

"Quentin, if something happens, all of your father's information is in my desk at my office in Santa Fe."

He snapped out of his musings. "Why? What's going to happen?"

"No. Nothing. I mean, you know, just in case. There is a demon who is quite prepared to kill us if we get in its way. I give us a fifty-fifty chance. If we make it through this, you can give me your address, and I'll send everything to you."

"No."

"No?" She frowned, the bite instantaneous. He didn't want her having his address? Was that it?

He pulled her onto his lap, and she settled against him. "No, I'm not leaving. Do you think I'm letting you go again?"

That sting in the backs of her eyes returned. After all these years...

"I just want to state for the record that if that demon kills me now, after all this time, after finally getting you back, I am going to be very angry."

A perfectly shaped brow arched heavenward. "Amber Kowalski, angry? I didn't realize such a thing was possible."

"Try leaving again without saying goodbye, and you'll find out just how angry I can get."

He snaked a hand up her T-shirt and over her rib cage, causing an outbreak of goose bumps to spread over her skin. "Is that a promise?" he asked.

"It's a threat."

"Ah."

"And not an idle one, either," she warned. "There is nothing idle about my threats. My threats are hardworking. Not afraid to get their hands dirty."

He laughed softly, the sound like a summer rain, and wrapped his arms around her. When he buried his face in the crook of her neck, she pulled him against her, and they held each other for a long moment, reveling in the feel, the perfect fit. The rightness. If they lived through the next few hours, she was so getting laid. Again.

Chapter Eleven

Visited hell.
Crazy shit went down.
Not allowed back.
—True story

Even after everything Quentin had put her through, Amber had still cared enough to search for his father. He didn't deserve her. He'd never deserved her. And yet, here she was. The elfin queen. Showering him with a love he'd craved for so long that he'd forgotten what it felt like to be happy. To be content.

As soon as this demon was dealt with, provided he survived, he was quitting La Guardia Segreta and going home. They wouldn't be thrilled about it, but they'd taken everything from him so he really didn't give a shit either way.

But first, he had a demon to see to.

He held onto the elfin for as long as he could. The feel of her both alleviating the agony inside him and aggravating it. He wanted more of her. Ached for more of her.

"*We have loved her for so long,*" Rune said.

"*I know.*" Rune had loved her through him. He'd known it for years.

"*This demon will not be easily defeated.*"

"*Are they ever?*" Quentin asked.

"*It will kill you to get to us.*"

"*That's not going to happen.*"

"*Precisely. You must release us. You must hand us over. We can be the distraction you need to get the upper hand.*"

"*Fuck off.*"

"*It's the only way.*"

"*It's too dangerous.*"

"*The demon is too fast, even for you.*"

"*Thanks for the vote of confidence.*"

"*I call 'em like I see 'em, human.*"

"*And how many of you will die in the process?*"

"*How many of you will die if we do not stop it?*"

In all the years Rune had been hitching a ride, Quentin never knew exactly who he was talking to. The leader, surely. But what was his name?

"*Don't go there, human.*"

Unfortunately, he couldn't have a single fucking thought without the whole of Rune knowing about it.

"*Exactly. So, stop thinking and kiss her again.*"

Quentin laughed. His relationship with the elfin could get awkward. Ménage à million. They'd have to deal with that later. For now, he asked anyway. "*What's your name?*"

"*What do you mean? We are Rune.*"

He pulled Amber tighter. "*If this goes south, I'd like to know who I've been talking to all this time.*"

"*You've been talking to Rune. We are one. We're like the Borg that way.*"

"*Really?* Star Trek *references?*"

"*Really.* Star Trek *references.*"

Okay, then. It would have to do for now. They had to get on with this before someone accidentally freed the demon. He loosened his hold, and Amber leaned back, her gaze so full of love it physically hurt. She had changed so much, and yet not at all. He brushed a thumb over her bow-shaped lips, and she leaned in and kissed him. He buried his hands in her hair and tilted his head to deepen the kiss. To breathe her in. To memorize her taste.

When she finished the kiss with several soft pecks over his face and drew back, a look of guilt had shadowed her features. "I'm sorry. About raking through your memories like that."

"Don't be. They've been left to their own devices for far too long. They probably needed to be raked. Maybe even weeded."

She laughed softly. "Are you ready?"

"As I'll ever be."

He pulled on an old canvas windbreaker and pushed the sleeves up to his elbows. A windbreaker with deep pockets that had been preloaded with black salt. She shrugged into the same jacket she'd worn before.

"I have a hoodie in there somewhere."

"No," she said, hugging the jacket to her. "I like this one."

"The rip down the center does give it that, what did you call it, *hobo* look?"

She giggled, the sound like sparkling water, and kissed him on the cheek. The fact that he'd never heard her giggle before today broke his heart. He'd been missing out.

"Let's go kick some demon ass," she said.

"Yeah, you get to stay in the truck, Rambo."

"What? I'm the one who told you about Sarah."

"You can help with her. Maybe knowing why all of this is happening will give us an edge. But when I have to face the demon, I need to know you're safe. Thinking otherwise will only distract me."

She blinked as she considered his words. "I guess. I certainly can't move like you can. But maybe it won't come to that. Maybe we can stop it through the website or whatever they're using to learn how to summon it, which, seriously, what the hell?"

"Maybe," he said, not believing that for a minute. "But I do agree. What the hell?"

"Can I bring the crossbow?"

"No."

They went back inside the Tavern and spotted their table. Kyle had come back in, and both he and Dora sat there, but the lunch crowd had cleared out. Most of them, anyway. The man in the Hawaiian shirt was still there, reading a paper.

Dora waved excitedly.

Kyle sent him a glare and asked. "You okay, boss?"

Amber gave him a thumbs-up just as Sarah saw them.

"You're back," she said as she wiped the table down. "I kept your food warm, but mostly you owe me forty bucks."

Quentin grinned. "Sorry. We had an emergency."

Sarah eyed Amber, clearly noting her change of clothes. Her mussed hair. Her pinkened cheeks. "I can see that."

Quentin took out a fifty and handed it to her as Amber asked, "Sarah, can we talk to you?"

She straightened in surprise. "Sure thing. Want to sit?" She gestured toward their table. The one that still had an old pair of sunglasses sitting on it. The ones Amber had put on Quentin. His eyes must've been black when she delved into his head. That would take some getting used to.

Instead of sitting in one of the empty seats, Sarah pulled up a fifth chair. Amber had been right. She *could* see Kyle and Dora, at least to some degree. They sat, and she looked between them, askance. "What's up?"

Quentin decided to leave the diplomacies to Amber. He'd never been good at tact.

"Sarah, did you summon a demon to kill Billy Tibbets, Angela Morrisey, and Dora Rodriguez?"

Okay, then. Maybe the elfin wasn't the best at diplomacy either.

Dora gasped and stared wide-eyed.

Sarah stilled for a long moment before sinking back in her chair.

A blonde woman came around the bar, combing through her bag as she walked toward the door. "I have a few errands to run. You okay for a bit, Sarah?"

Sarah nodded, her response automated.

The woman stopped and studied the group curiously. "Is everything okay?"

Sarah snapped out of it and turned to her. "It's all good, Lori. We're just catching up."

Not entirely convinced given the look on her face, the woman pulled the strap over her shoulder and headed out. "I won't be long."

Sarah waved and then turned back to them. "I don't know what you're talking about."

"Of course, you do. We know it was you. We just don't know how. Or why."

She crossed her arms over her chest. "What does it matter? It's not like you can prosecute me for summoning a demon."

Dora made the sign of the cross.

Amber tilted her head in thought. "Technically true. But you need to be honest with us. Did you sic it on anyone else?"

She pressed her lips together to fight a grin, then shook her head. "No. Is that who's here?" She pointed to the only two departed people in the room. "Are they going to haunt me or something?"

"Dora's here," Amber said. "Billy and Angela must've crossed over."

Sarah laughed and shook her head. "So, they get to go to heaven? Is that it?"

Quentin noted her distaste. "You didn't want them to?"

"No. I did not want them to bask in eternal bliss. If that's even real."

Amber leaned forward. "Sarah, what did they do? Dora honestly doesn't know."

"The fuck she doesn't." The woman Quentin had once thought so pretty became little more than a demon herself in his eyes. Ugly with hatred and vitriol.

Dora pressed both hands to her chest. "I don't understand, Amber. I don't even know her. What could I have done to her to make her hate me so much?"

Amber turned back to Sarah. "She doesn't know you. What is it you think she did?"

A cryptic smile spread across the woman's face. One filtered through resentment and cruelty. "Madeline Kemp."

Dora's expression morphed from confusion to doubt then finally to realization. "She's Madeline? The little girl who disappeared on my bus route? But that was…that was over twenty years ago." She clasped her hands at her mouth. "She's alive? All this time, she's been alive?"

Quentin and Amber watched as Dora's emotions ran the gamut. At first, she was filled with joy, thrilled that the little girl who'd disappeared years ago was alive and well. Then the stark reality hit her. The fact that Sarah hated her so much that she'd summoned a demon to kill her. Tears pooled between her lashes.

"What happened, Sarah?" Amber asked.

"I was abducted that day, and that bitch knows it."

Dora shook her head. "I don't understand how she could believe such a thing."

"You were abducted?"

"Of course, I was abducted. And my own mother set it up."

Amber seemed taken aback. "How do you know?"

"Because I found the letters between her and the Gladwells."

"The Gladwells?"

"The couple who abducted me. They told me my mother was sick and I had to go live with them. But my mother practically sold me to that crazy old couple as cheap labor."

"No," Dora said. "Pauline would never do that. And she really was sick. She died of cancer not long after Madeline disappeared."

"Wait." Amber held up a hand in a timeout. "What does any of this have to do with Billy and Angela?"

"It was all their fault. They lied to everyone. Said they saw me skinning a coyote."

"Were you?"

"Yes, but they said it was still alive."

Amber raised her chin, clearly upset by the thought. "Was it?"

The woman scoffed. "How is that even remotely relevant?"

"You thought they deserved to die because they lied about a coyote?"

"They also said I broke a little girl's arm."

"Did you?"

Sarah glared at her. "She took my doll. Damn straight, I did."

"*Ay, Dios mio*," Dora said. "Pauline was afraid of her. She tried to tell me, but… I just couldn't imagine it."

Amber went to grab the woman's hand, then remembered she couldn't. "I saw Dora's memories, Sarah. I don't know what you think happened, or how you think she was involved, but she did her job correctly. The cattle guard was down. She couldn't get across."

"It was a setup. I know damned well she was in on it. The cattle guard just happened to be down when the Gladwells were waiting for me? Not likely."

Amber leaned forward. "Did they…were you hurt?"

"No. They just kept me on the farm. Didn't let me go to school or have any friends. I… They died when I was sixteen. That's when I found the letters. My mother set it all up. Said she was worried I would hurt someone."

"How did they die?"

"That's not the point!" Sarah slammed a hand on the table.

Amber blanched, and Quentin almost came unglued. He steeled himself, biding his time.

"No, I don't suppose it is," Amber said.

"*Ay, Dios mio*," Dora repeated, then hugged herself and rocked.

"Are you okay, hon?" Amber asked her.

"What's she saying?" Sarah asked. "How is she here?"

Quentin scrubbed his face. "This still doesn't tell us how you did it."

"Thinking about using it yourself?"

Amber pressed her nails into the palms of her hands and drew blood. It disturbed him, but she was focused on the psychopath in front of her. "You need to tell us, Sarah."

"Why?"

"Because the demon doesn't just kill the people you summoned it for. It kills the summoner, too."

She stilled. "You're fucking with me."

"It's a tad angry about being controlled."

The fear on her face was genuine. "Yeah, but it's not just me. Lots of people have used it."

"Yes, and they've all died," Quentin said.

She looked at him. "Are you even Deaf, or was that a ruse, too?"

"Sarah, how did you contact it?" Amber asked. "How did you summon it?"

"On the dark web. There's a group that worships this demon named Sadeet. For five hundred bucks, they tell you how to summon it. How to basically get away with murder."

Quentin took out his phone. "I'll let La Guardia know. They can take down the site and figure out who's behind it so they don't do something like this again with another demon."

"And how will they do that?" Amber asked. "Considering how gentle they were with you."

He looked up at her, surprised. "You're worried about the people who sell an all-access pass to a demon assassin?"

"No." She crossed her arms. "I guess not."

"*The house, human,*" Rune said.

Quentin watched through Rune's eyes. Someone, a girl, opened the front door of Dora's house. She pushed the salt aside.

"*Get ready,*" Rune said. *"It's coming."*

Quentin retrieved the dagger from the sheath he'd slipped into the back of his pants. He felt rather than saw the tendrils of ink slide across his eyes and slowly fill them. Unable to help that now, he took Amber by the arm and lifted her out of the chair. "It's coming."

"What?" Startled, she glanced around.

"My niece," Dora said, looking out the window.

"She broke the circle." He shoved her toward the door. "Get out. Get inside my truck. It's protected."

"*Release us, human.*"

"No."

"*You will not survive.*"

Quentin drew in a deep breath and said out loud, "You fucking say that every time."

"And one day, we will be right."

"Yeah, well, today's not that day."

"Quentin?" Amber said.

He pulled her to him with one arm, keeping the dagger far away from her. It was much sharper than it looked and infused with an ancient and powerful curse. One slice could kill her. Or him, for that matter.

Despite his eyes, she rose onto her tiptoes, cupped his face, and pressed her mouth to his.

The kiss was magical. He drew power from it. Energy and warmth and light. Like the electric company, only hotter. Much, much hotter.

With a reluctance forfeited by urgency, he broke off the kiss, pressed his mouth to her ear, and whispered, "Run."

Chapter Twelve

Of course, I have flaws,
but my boobs usually distract people from them.
—T-shirt

His bravery was staggering. Amber had never been more in love in her life. There simply weren't many men in the world who would risk facing a demon just to save a few people. A few people he did not know and would never meet.

He wrapped a hand around the back of her head and pulled her close, his mouth warm at her ear as he whispered, "Run."

She'd used the kiss as a distraction and grabbed some of the salt from his pocket. She put it into her jacket and nodded. "Sarah, come on."

"There's a back door," she said, suddenly willing to cooperate if it meant saving her sociopathic ass.

"Hawaii," Amber said since he was the only one left in the Tavern. "Time to go."

He'd been paying attention. He folded the paper and followed them without question.

Sarah led them through the kitchen and toward the back, but Amber stopped. "You guys run. Hawaii—"

"Steve."

"Steve, whatever you do, don't follow Sarah."

"You got it." He hurried out the back exit, his flip-flops slapping the wood floor. Sun streamed in when he opened the door. Little man could run.

She turned to Sarah. "Go."

"I thought…you have to protect me."

"The only person who can protect you is in the dining area, and I'm not leaving him."

Sarah grabbed a knife. "Yes, you are."

"Really?" Amber asked. Sociopaths sucked.

When a thundering bang shook the building, Sarah gasped, her eyes wide with fear.

The cook stopped cleaning up and looked around.

"You need to leave," Amber said to him.

Dora appeared, pointing toward the front. "It's here, *Madre de Dios.*"

The cook looked around. "What the hell?"

"You need to leave," Amber repeated.

"Come on, Sarah," he said when another loud crash sounded. This time, chairs had been upended. The demon was not happy, and Quentin was in there with it. Alone.

Amber took the opportunity to run to the swinging door between the dining area and the kitchen. She looked out the small window. The room looked as if a tornado had hit it, and Quentin stood there waiting as he basically watched the demon throw a temper tantrum.

Then he was hit. He crashed through the door, taking her with him. They landed in a heap by the refrigeration units. The demon came barreling through the double doors, clearly hurt. Even angrier. Quentin had gotten it with the salt again.

Sarah stood staring at the creature. It was solid, so she got a very good view of what she had summoned. She couldn't move. Fear had frozen her to the spot. She only looked up at it, her jaw hanging open.

Amber and Quentin scrambled to their feet as the demon spotted its summoner.

"I thought I told you to run," Quentin said over his shoulder. He took the lead and kept himself between Amber and the demon.

"I did run. Just not very far." Amber checked the area. The cook was gone, thank God.

The demon took a step closer to Sarah, its claw scraping on the wood floor. But with each step, the floor faded away, and another dimension appeared beneath its feet. The other dimension spread, its energy building and twisting around them until they were standing in the funnel of a tornado.

"Stay behind me!" Quentin yelled, but Amber pushed past him as the demon bore down on Sarah.

"She didn't know you were real!" she said to it, hoping to reason with it.

It spared her a quick glance, but before Amber could process what was happening, it pounced on Sarah and swallowed her whole.

Amber gasped. Her hands flew to her mouth as the demon looked at her and uttered in a guttural, gravelly voice, "She does now."

The demon swung. Its claw caught Quentin across the chest, but Quentin cut its talon with the dagger. The demon let loose an unearthly screech. It bought them some time.

As Quentin doubled over, blood soaking his T-shirt alarmingly fast, Amber covered him with her body, reached into her pocket, and released salt into the wind.

The entity screamed, and the dimension fell away, but it wouldn't stop the demon for long. She had to get Quentin out of there. The demon had done what it set out to do. It'd killed the summoner. Surely, it would just leave. Instead, it turned toward them, its eyes glistening as its tongue slithered out.

"No, goddammit," Quentin said, almost to himself. He was talking to Rune. Arguing with him.

And Amber realized that Rune was likely trying to talk Quentin into releasing them to the demon. To feed it. Rune knew the demon would kill Quentin to get to them.

Just then, someone shouted from behind it. "Hey!"

The demon turned, and they all saw Kyle standing there, pointing his pen at it.

"Get away from them!"

It was the opening Quentin had been waiting for. He vaulted over Amber, landed on the demon's head, and used all of his weight to flip it onto its back.

They crushed the prep station and took out half the ceiling in the process. Sheetrock and paint snowed down on them as Quentin jumped on top of the demon and pressed a knee into its throat. But the demon was too strong. With one swipe, it could take Quentin out for good.

Amber reacted without thought. She scrambled to the demon and straightened onto her knees over its head.

It couldn't help it. It spared her a glance.

It was all she needed. She *dove*. She let the world fall away around them and dove into its mind, paralyzing it.

"Tra-vel-er," it croaked, completely helpless. "What are you doing?"

Quentin answered for her. "The compass or the knife?"

She could see in her periphery that he held the dagger perpendicular to the demon's heart with one hand, and the compass in the other, but he was fading fast. Blood flowed from him in rivers. It pooled onto the demon's chest, and Amber almost lost her concentration.

"The compass or the knife?" he repeated, his eyes as black as a moonless night.

Amber bounced back and kept it paralyzed as she plundered its memories. Someone, it didn't know who, had figured out how to summon it. It didn't want to leave the plane until it found out who, but it would have little choice now.

Quentin sank the knife into its chest just a fraction of an inch, and it screamed again, but only in its mind. Amber had paralyzed its vocal cords. It was so hungry. It just wanted to eat.

"Compass," it said to her with its mind.

"I am going to release you. If you do anything other than go into the compass, you will die. Painfully. I will see to it myself."

"Traveler," it said almost lovingly.

She released it, and it dematerialized just as Quentin opened the compass. He turned the face, and a burst of light exploded from it. He held it steady and waited. Even if the demon had changed its mind, the compass would've captured him, and she realized it was another dimension. With four jewels on it, it could actually be four dimensions, probably each inescapable. Hopefully, once there, the demon could no longer be summoned onto this plane.

They would have to figure out who'd started it all before he or she found another demon to do their bidding.

When the blinding light dissipated, Quentin closed the compass and sank to his knees. Amber caught him just in time for them both to faceplant on the floor.

Chapter Thirteen

If you get in my car, then you've just
won a free ticket to see me live and in concert.
—True story

"It's a coffee shop. Talk to Charley. She'll get you across."

"Thank you," Dora said to Amber. Quentin watched them, but they were sitting in front of a window with a large, orange sun behind them. It was so bright he could only see their silhouettes. "I'd like to say goodbye to my family. Would that be possible?"

"She'll help you with that, too."

"Thank you for everything, Amber. I wish I could hug you."

Amber clasped her hands at her chest. "I do, too."

"Take care of him." Dora gestured toward Quentin just as he saw the IV and realized where he was.

He bolted upright. He could not be in a hospital. Not with how fast he healed.

"Quentin!" Amber said. Dora disappeared, and Amber lunged at him. "What are you doing? Lay back."

"I can't be here," he said, pushing at the blankets.

"Relax. We're in my apartment. We have a lovely doctor who's...friendly to our cause. She came over and got some blood into you since you decided to ditch what you had in Madrid. And now, she's just trying to rehydrate you."

He sank back onto the pillows.

"You good, boss?" Kyle asked from the doorway.

"I am. Thank you, Kyle."

When the man glanced at him, Quentin nodded a greeting. Kyle offered him a sheepish smile and disappeared. The nerd had come through. If not for him, the day could've ended badly. Or, well, worse.

"So," Amber said, tugging her Betty Boop comforter tight again, "the Vatican is looking into the website. They've already taken it down and are searching for the person who started it."

"And you know this because…?"

"I contacted them. Using your phone, of course. I told them what happened with the demon and gave them your two-weeks' notice, starting two weeks ago." She sat beside him on the bed and felt his forehead, her fingers cool against his blistering skin. She'd braided her long hair and wore a T-shirt and boxers as if she were just getting ready for bed. Or waking up. She looked as fresh as morning dew either way.

"How long have I been here?"

"Only a few hours. You weren't kidding. You heal fast. I was just getting ready to get some sleep when my mom called. She's bringing over soup."

He winced. "Does she hate me?"

Amber cupped his face. Ran her thumb over his unshaven jaw. Looked at him like he'd hung the moon. If she only knew how wrong she was. He could only imagine how bad he looked. She didn't seem to care. "She could never hate you. My stepdad, however, is a little miffed."

"Great."

She laughed softly. "They love you, Quentin. Nothing will change that."

"And you?"

She swung her legs up onto the bed and sat cross-legged. "What about me?"

He chuckled, then asked in alarm, "Wait, how did you get me here?"

The grin she flashed him stole his breath. "Remember Hawaii? Steve?"

"You're kidding."

"Nope. We owe that man dinner. Or possibly a small island. He helped me get you to the truck and then drove my car while I drove you."

He shook his head. "Why?"

"Apparently, he is a fan of the supernatural."

"Nice. What about the Tavern?"

"I'm still waiting to hear. We got out of there pretty fast, but the whole town heard the commotion. We'll probably get a bill any day now. Or arrested. It's hard to say."

His gaze traveled the length of her. "It'll be worth it."

* * * *

Amber watched as he took her in, giddy about the fact that he even wanted to. After all this time, Quentin Rutherford was back in her life. But she didn't want to make a big deal about it, to pressure him, so she changed the subject. "I can't get over how well you know English now."

"Rune. Yammering in my head ad nauseam."

"Was it just me, or were you embarrassed to speak to me at first?"

"I was, yes." He looked away. "I don't sound right."

She brushed a lock of hair off his brow. "You sound perfect."

"But you can still tell I'm Deaf."

"You can still tell you have hearing loss. Is that bad? I mean, you used to speak a word here and there all the time. You were never embarrassed before."

"I'd never heard my voice before."

In her head, she said, *You mean the panty-melting, bone-dissolving, orgasm-inducing voice that she would never grow tired of hearing?* Out loud, she said, "Oh, I see."

"You called it Q&A Investigations."

"What?" She was still on the panty-melting portion of the program.

"Your business. You named it after the business we started in high school."

"I did. It seemed appropriate."

"Amber." He took her hand. "You could've become anything. Why are you a PI?"

"What's wrong with being a PI?"

"Nothing. It's just... You're so smart."

"You thought I would become a doctor or a lawyer or something."

"Something like that."

"I had a calling. What can I say? I wanted to follow in Aunt Charley's footsteps."

His gaze landed on her mouth and stayed there. "When is your mom going to be here?"

"Probably any minute."

"How much time do you think we have?"

"Probably not much."

He nodded in disappointment.

"No," she said, snuggling beside him, "I mean, we should hurry."

"Oh. Right. Okay, then." He sent a hand under the waistband of her boxers.

"Wait," she said, stopping it from reaching the motherland. "What does Rune do when you...when we...you know?"

"Shouldn't you have thought of that before?"

"Hardly the point."

He filled his lungs. "I won't lie to you, Amber. He's kind of a part of it." When she only stared at him, he sank back onto the pillows. "I don't even know where I stop and he starts anymore."

She couldn't imagine how he felt. To have something inside you that could take control like that. And she'd sicced Rune on him. Forced Quentin to stand down.

"I don't blame you if you don't want to have sex ever again."

"Please." She propped herself up, gazed into his eyes, and then delved into his mind. "Rune, look away."

Hundreds of thousands of Rune-ians—Rune-ites?—turned away from her in unison. "Wow, did you know the citizens of Rune all have these long, curved spikes on their backs?"

"Yeah, I don't care," Quentin said, right before attacking.

He really did recover fast.

* * * *

Also from 1001 Dark Nights and Darynda Jones, discover The Graveyard Shift.

Sign up for the 1001 Dark Nights Newsletter
and be entered to win a Tiffany Key necklace.

There's a contest every month!

Go to www.1001DarkNights.com to subscribe.

**As a bonus, all subscribers can download
FIVE FREE exclusive books!**

Discover 1001 Dark Nights Collection Eight

DRAGON REVEALED by Donna Grant
A Dragon Kings Novella

CAPTURED IN INK by Carrie Ann Ryan
A Montgomery Ink: Boulder Novella

SECURING JANE by Susan Stoker
A SEAL of Protection: Legacy Series Novella

WILD WIND by Kristen Ashley
A Chaos Novella

DARE TO TEASE by Carly Phillips
A Dare Nation Novella

VAMPIRE by Rebecca Zanetti
A Dark Protectors/Rebels Novella

MAFIA KING by Rachel Van Dyken
A Mafia Royals Novella

THE GRAVEDIGGER'S SON by Darynda Jones
A Charley Davidson Novella

FINALE by Skye Warren
A North Security Novella

MEMORIES OF YOU by J. Kenner
A Stark Securities Novella

SLAYED BY DARKNESS by Alexandra Ivy
A Guardians of Eternity Novella

TREASURED by Lexi Blake
A Masters and Mercenaries Novella

THE DAREDEVIL by Dylan Allen
A Rivers Wilde Novella

BOND OF DESTINY by Larissa Ione
A Demonica Novella

THE CLOSE-UP by Kennedy Ryan
A Hollywood Renaissance Novella

MORE THAN POSSESS YOU by Shayla Black
A More Than Words Novella

HAUNTED HOUSE by Heather Graham
A Krewe of Hunters Novella

MAN FOR ME by Laurelin Paige
A Man In Charge Novella

THE RHYTHM METHOD by Kylie Scott
A Stage Dive Novella

JONAH BENNETT by Tijan
A Bennett Mafia Novella

CHANGE WITH ME by Kristen Proby
A With Me In Seattle Novella

THE DARKEST DESTINY by Gena Showalter
A Lords of the Underworld Novella

Also from Blue Box Press

THE LAST TIARA by M.J. Rose

THE CROWN OF GILDED BONES by Jennifer L. Armentrout
A Blood and Ash Novel

THE MISSING SISTER by Lucinda Riley

Discover More Darynda Jones

The Graveyard Shift
A Charley Davidson Novella

Guarding a precocious five-year-old who is half-human, half-god, and 100% destined to save the world is no easy feat.

Garrett Swopes was the ultimate skeptic until he met a certain hellion and her husband. They vanished after stopping a catastrophic event and left him, a mere mortal, in charge of protecting their gift to mankind. But when she disappears as well, he needs the help of another breed of hellion. One who can see past the veil of space and time. One who betrayed him.

She will get a truce in the deal, but she will never earn his forgiveness.

Marika Dubois's son—a warrior in the coming war between heaven and hell—was foreseen long before his birth. But to create a child strong enough to endure the trials that lay ahead, she needed a descendant of powerful magics. She found that in Garrett Swopes and tricked him into fathering her son. A ploy he has never forgiven her for. But when he knocks on her door asking for her help, she sees the fierce attraction he tries to deny rise within him.

And Marika has to decide if she dares risk her heart a second time to help the only man she's ever loved.

* * * *

Charley Davidson, a god with a penchant for maiming first and asking questions later, was going to kill Garrett. No, that wasn't right. Charley's husband, Reyes Farrow, also a god with a penchant for maiming first and asking questions later, would start the whole process by ripping him to shreds, then letting Charley finish him off. Gladly. And with much glee.

Garrett had one job. One. Fucking. Job. Watch his best friends' daughter, Beep, aka Elwyn Alexandra Loehr, a kid who just happened to be destined to save the world from a catastrophic demon uprising. He was supposed to guard her with his life. To keep her safe. To protect her from all the ghosts and goblins—metaphorically speaking since he didn't have a supernatural bone in his body—hell-bent on doing her harm before she could prevent said catastrophic demon uprising.

He failed.

Yesterday, at exactly 3:33 p.m., the precocious five-year-old was running across a sun-drenched field of sagebrush and wild grasses when she disappeared right before his eyes. One second she was tripping over, well, absolutely nothing—so much like her mother, it startled him—and the next, she was gone.

If he hadn't been looking right at her, if his gaze hadn't been laser-locked on the long, dark tangles cascading down her back, if she hadn't disappeared between his strategically placed blinks, he would've questioned the entire event. But there was simply no doubt about it. She'd vanished into thin air.

The way she disappeared would suggest a supernatural influence, especially considering the fact that she was the daughter of two gods, but her celestial parents had placed a shield over the entire area. No supernatural entity could penetrate it. Was there some loophole they'd missed? Some escape clause they'd overlooked?

Garrett didn't hesitate. He immediately called in his entire team, but even his most preternaturally enhanced members couldn't figure out what had happened, and one of them was a bona fide angel. Well, former angel.

After thirty-six hours of scouring every inch of Santa Fe and the surrounding area for even a sign of the little hellion, a storm had rolled in, and the search had to be abandoned. Garrett left his team at the compound, as well as the Loehrs, Elwyn's grandparents, panicked and scrambling to figure out what'd happened. In the meantime, he went in search of the only woman he knew who could see past the veil of not only space, but time as well.

He had one clue to go on. Elwyn's last words before she took off across the rugged New Mexican terrain.

Surely, he'd heard her wrong. He prayed he'd heard her wrong as he fought the winds and icy pelts of the desert storm, then raised a fist and pounded on the door of his ex, Marika Dubois.

About Darynda Jones

NY Times and *USA Today* Bestselling Author Darynda Jones has won numerous awards for her work, including a prestigious RITA, a Golden Heart, and a Daphne du Maurier, and her books have been translated into 18 languages. As a born storyteller, Darynda grew up spinning tales of dashing damsels and heroes in distress for any unfortunate soul who happened by, and she is ever so grateful for the opportunity to carry on that legacy. She currently has two series with St. Martin's Press: The Charley Davidson Series and the Darklight Trilogy. She lives in the Land of Enchantment, also known as New Mexico, with her husband and two beautiful sons, the Mighty, Mighty Jones Boys.

She can be found at http://www.daryndajones.com

Discover 1001 Dark Nights

TRICKED by Rebecca Zanetti ~ DIRTY WICKED by Shayla Black ~ THE ONLY ONE by Lauren Blakely ~ SWEET SURRENDER by Liliana Hart

COLLECTION FOUR
ROCK CHICK REAWAKENING by Kristen Ashley ~ ADORING INK by Carrie Ann Ryan ~ SWEET RIVALRY by K. Bromberg ~ SHADE'S LADY by Joanna Wylde ~ RAZR by Larissa Ione ~ ARRANGED by Lexi Blake ~ TANGLED by Rebecca Zanetti ~ HOLD ME by J. Kenner ~ SOMEHOW, SOME WAY by Jennifer Probst ~ TOO CLOSE TO CALL by Tessa Bailey ~ HUNTED by Elisabeth Naughton ~ EYES ON YOU by Laura Kaye ~ BLADE by Alexandra Ivy/Laura Wright ~ DRAGON BURN by Donna Grant ~ TRIPPED OUT by Lorelei James ~ STUD FINDER by Lauren Blakely ~ MIDNIGHT UNLEASHED by Lara Adrian ~ HALLOW BE THE HAUNT by Heather Graham ~ DIRTY FILTHY FIX by Laurelin Paige ~ THE BED MATE by Kendall Ryan ~ NIGHT GAMES by CD Reiss ~ NO RESERVATIONS by Kristen Proby ~ DAWN OF SURRENDER by Liliana Hart

COLLECTION FIVE
BLAZE ERUPTING by Rebecca Zanetti ~ ROUGH RIDE by Kristen Ashley ~ HAWKYN by Larissa Ione ~ RIDE DIRTY by Laura Kaye ~ ROME'S CHANCE by Joanna Wylde ~ THE MARRIAGE ARRANGEMENT by Jennifer Probst ~ SURRENDER by Elisabeth Naughton ~ INKED NIGHTS by Carrie Ann Ryan ~ ENVY by Rachel Van Dyken ~ PROTECTED by Lexi Blake ~ THE PRINCE by Jennifer L. Armentrout ~ PLEASE ME by J. Kenner ~ WOUND TIGHT by Lorelei James ~ STRONG by Kylie Scott ~ DRAGON NIGHT by Donna Grant ~ TEMPTING BROOKE by Kristen Proby ~ HAUNTED BE THE HOLIDAYS by Heather Graham ~ CONTROL by K. Bromberg ~ HUNKY HEARTBREAKER by Kendall Ryan ~ THE DARKEST CAPTIVE by Gena Showalter

COLLECTION SIX
DRAGON CLAIMED by Donna Grant ~ ASHES TO INK by Carrie Ann Ryan ~ ENSNARED by Elisabeth Naughton ~ EVERMORE by Corinne Michaels ~ VENGEANCE by Rebecca Zanetti ~ ELI'S TRIUMPH by Joanna Wylde ~ CIPHER by Larissa Ione ~

RESCUING MACIE by Susan Stoker ~ ENCHANTED by Lexi Blake ~ TAKE THE BRIDE by Carly Phillips ~ INDULGE ME by J. Kenner ~ THE KING by Jennifer L. Armentrout ~ QUIET MAN by Kristen Ashley ~ ABANDON by Rachel Van Dyken ~ THE OPEN DOOR by Laurelin Paige ~ CLOSER by Kylie Scott ~ SOMETHING JUST LIKE THIS by Jennifer Probst ~ BLOOD NIGHT by Heather Graham ~ TWIST OF FATE by Jill Shalvis ~ MORE THAN PLEASURE YOU by Shayla Black ~ WONDER WITH ME by Kristen Proby ~ THE DARKEST ASSASSIN by Gena Showalter

COLLECTION SEVEN
THE BISHOP by Skye Warren ~ TAKEN WITH YOU by Carrie Ann Ryan ~ DRAGON LOST by Donna Grant ~ SEXY LOVE by Carly Phillips ~ PROVOKE by Rachel Van Dyken ~ RAFE by Sawyer Bennett ~ THE NAUGHTY PRINCESS by Claire Contreras ~ THE GRAVEYARD SHIFT by Darynda Jones ~ CHARMED by Lexi Blake ~ SACRIFICE OF DARKNESS by Alexandra Ivy ~ THE QUEEN by Jen Armentrout ~ BEGIN AGAIN by Jennifer Probst ~ VIXEN by Rebecca Zanetti ~ SLASH by Laurelin Paige ~ THE DEAD HEAT OF SUMMER by Heather Graham ~ WILD FIRE by Kristen Ashley ~ MORE THAN PROTECT YOU by Shayla Black ~ LOVE SONG by Kylie Scott ~ CHERISH ME by J. Kenner ~ SHINE WITH ME by Kristen Proby

Discover Blue Box Press
TAME ME by J. Kenner ~ TEMPT ME by J. Kenner ~ DAMIEN by J. Kenner ~ TEASE ME by J. Kenner ~ REAPER by Larissa Ione ~ THE SURRENDER GATE by Christopher Rice ~ SERVICING THE TARGET by Cherise Sinclair ~ THE LAKE OF LEARNING by Steve Berry and MJ Rose ~ THE MUSEUM OF MYSTERIES by Steve Berry and MJ Rose ~ TEASE ME by J. Kenner ~ FROM BLOOD AND ASH by Jennifer L. Armentrout ~ QUEEN MOVE by Kennedy Ryan ~ THE HOUSE OF LONG AGO by Steve Berry and MJ Rose ~ THE BUTTERFLY ROOM by Lucinda Riley ~ A KINGDOM OF FLESH AND FIRE by Jennifer L. Armentrout

On Behalf of 1001 Dark Nights,

Liz Berry, M.J. Rose, and Jillian Stein would like to thank ~

Steve Berry
Doug Scofield
Benjamin Stein
Kim Guidroz
Social Butterfly PR
Ashley Wells
Asha Hossain
Chris Graham
Chelle Olson
Kasi Alexander
Jessica Johns
Dylan Stockton
Richard Blake
and Simon Lipskar

Made in the USA
Las Vegas, NV
08 May 2021